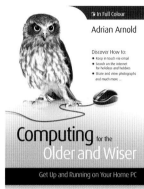
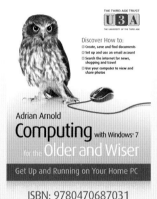

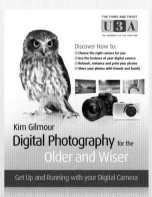
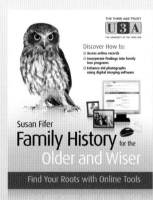

THE MYSTERY AT KINGSLEY HALL

The Mystery At Kingsley Hall

by

Shirley Worrall

Dales Large Print Books
Long Preston, North Yorkshire,
BD23 4ND, England.

British Library Cataloguing in Publication Data.

Worrall, Shirley
    The mystery at Kingsley Hall.

    A catalogue record of this book is
    available from the British Library

    ISBN   978-1-84262-543-9 pbk

First published in Great Britain by D.C. Thomson

Copyright © Shirley Worrall

Cover illustration © Len Thurston by arrangement with
P.W.A. International Ltd.

The moral right of the author has been asserted

Published in Large Print 2007 by arrangement with
Shirley Worrall, care of Dorian Literary Agency

Dales Large Print is an imprint of Library Magna Books Ltd.

Printed and bound in Great Britain by
T.J. (International) Ltd., Cornwall, PL28 8RW

CHAPTER ONE

'Over here, Des!'

Laurie Summerfield spotted him as soon as he pushed open the door, and waved to attract his attention.

Des looked a little embarrassed as he wove his way through the crowded coffee bar to the table.

'With a greeting like that, everyone will think I'm your sugar daddy!'

Laura laughed. Des Turner had been her tutor at horticultural college, and now he was her friend. They met perhaps a dozen times a year, and it was always a pleasure to see him.

She very much doubted that people would see them as a couple. At fifty-two, twice Laurie's age, he had too much the air of the family man about him, which was exactly what Des was. He was devoted to his lovely wife and their four grown children.

'In that case, you'll have to pay. I'm sure it's your turn anyway,' Laurie said.

'On my salary? You're the one coining it in, thanks to my expertise.'

They were still laughing when the waitress came over.

Laurie, having been there far too early, had already had a cappuccino. She ordered another, as well as the chocolate mousse she'd had her eye on since she'd walked in. Des ordered apple pie and ice-cream to go with his coffee.

'The prices they charge for a coffee.' He shook his head. 'You should have come to our place – Fran could give you a jar full of the stuff for that price!'

'And how is the poor woman?' Laurie grinned. 'She hasn't traded you in for a well-behaved version yet?'

'She'd never cope without me.' He smiled affectionately. 'She's fine, thanks. As lovely as ever.'

'And the kids?'

'How would I know? They're far too busy to let their parents know what they're doing!'

She laughed.

'What about you, Laurie? How's your dad – better than the last time we spoke, I hope?'

'Oh, he's fine,' she said, just as she always did. 'The bronchitis cleared up.'

'Not that I've seen much of him lately,' she went on, eager to change the subject. 'I've been far too busy working.'

'The hospice?'

'Yes.' Designing the gardens for the local hospice had been her most prestigious, as well as her most rewarding, job yet. 'Did I show you my plans?'

'Only a dozen times.'

'Well, I'm pleased with it. It's peaceful, calming, soothing – I love it. And so do the patients.'

'And what's next?'

The waitress put their order in front of them.

'I don't know,' Laurie admitted. 'I've got a couple of possibilities, but nothing I'm excited about.'

'Good, because I've got something to put to you.'

Happy to keep her guessing, Des sampled his apple pie.

'Almost as good as Fran makes!'

'Never mind that,' Laurie teased. 'What do you have to put to me?'

'There's a man in Lancashire – or is it Yorkshire? Lancashire, I think. Anyway, a chap there wants his garden designing.'

Laurie felt a moment's disappointment. It was Des who'd put her on to the hospice project, and she'd expected something bigger, something more challenging.

'As soon as he described the place, I thought of you.'

'What sort of place is it?' Laurie asked.

'Big.'

Even a big garden didn't excite her. Thanks to the deluge of gardening programmes on TV these days, she suspected the usual decking and paving would be required.

'Do you remember those designs you did – for the stately home – when you first came to college?'

'The ones you said were ridiculously self-indulgent?'

'Yeah, those. From what this chap says, his place would suit those designs to a T.'

Now Laurie's interest was sparked.

'When you say big, Des, how big are you talking?'

'Oh, about five hundred acres, if I remember correctly.' He laughed at the shocked expression on her face.

'Don't get too excited, though,' he warned. 'There's a deer park, too. Is the deer park included or not? Can't remember. Anyway, we're talking stately home. Apparently, this chap's been out of the country for twenty years and has returned to the ancestral home to find a wilderness waiting. He's a bit strapped for cash, I gather, so he wants to open the place to the public.'

'Is that so?' If Laurie didn't get this job, she would be bitterly disappointed. 'Tell me more.'

'I gather there are terraces, a lake–'

'No! Tell me how I get this job!'

'I thought he'd want to talk over his plans with a few designers,' Des explained, 'but he seems happy to accept my judgement, so I said I had someone in mind. You'd need to talk it over with him, see what he wants, tell him what would work and what wouldn't, and then it would be up to him.'

'Send me!' she begged.

'I'll give him a call on Monday and fix something up,' he promised, laughing at her excitement. 'It would mean living on site, of course. Still, you're from that neck of the woods, aren't you?'

'How would I know? You're not even sure if it's in Lancashire or Yorkshire!'

Des thought for a moment.

'Lancashire,' he decided. 'Right on the border. Pennines. I had a look at the map after I'd spoken to him. It's not far from Rochdale.'

Laurie's heart skipped oddly.

'Some hall or other,' Des went on. 'Ah, Kingsley Hall!'

Laurie's heartbeat seemed to stop altogether.

'What's the man's name?'

But she knew. She also knew that Des had been wasting his breath about this job.

'Quite an ordinary surname,' Des said, trying to think. 'Called himself Toby.'

'Davis?' she suggested, her throat dry.

'That's it! Toby Davis!'

Tobias William Charles Marchington-Davis, to give him his full name... Des was looking at her curiously.

'Do you know the place?'

'I know of it,' she replied, swallowing hard.

11

Kingsley Hall, with its lake, terracing and deer park, had been home for the first eight years of Laurie's life, not that Des knew that. Few people did.

It was almost twenty years ago now – November 5, 1985, Bonfire Night – the irony of that never escaped her. That was when her whole world had disintegrated around her.

'So are you still interested?' Des asked. 'Only you look a bit – disappointed.'

'Well, the thing is–'

What could she say? How could she tell Des that his Toby Davis wouldn't allow her within sight of his precious home?

'Yes, of course I'm interested.' She dragged up a smile. 'It's a – lovely place. Well, from what I've heard. Yes, I'm interested. Is it this Toby who wants to talk to me?'

'Yes.'

There was no point taking the matter any further, then. She would be the last person on earth Toby Davis would employ. How could she explain that, though?

She played with her coffee for a few moments, trying to think, trying not to remember.

After all, there was no reason why Toby would connect twenty-six-year-old Laurie Summerfield with the gangly Laura Whitney he'd once known. She'd been eight when the family had been banished from Kingsley Hall in disgrace. Toby had been – what? He

12

must have been thirteen.

Since then Laurie had grown up, married, divorced amicably, and begun a career she loved.

Toby wouldn't recognise her, of that she was certain. But – could she bear to go back?

She thought longingly of the house and grounds. She'd always believed – still did probably – that there was no more beautiful place on earth than Kingsley Hall. She'd known and loved every inch of it, house and grounds.

'So when shall I tell him you'll be free to go up there?'

Laurie pushed the memories aside, took her diary from her bag, and scribbled down a few dates she couldn't make during the next month.

It was foolish to turn down the chance of a look at her old home. Besides, what harm could it do?'

'Right, out with it!' Sheena and Laurie might only have known each other for four years, but they were more like sisters than flatmates. 'Something's bothering you.' She had a sudden worry. 'It's not your dad, is it?'

'No. Well, not really.'

Sheena sighed, put the last of the plates away and filled the kettle.

'Is it or isn't it? Are you visiting him this afternoon?'

'Of course,' Laurie smiled. 'I always do on Sundays.' She nodded at the kettle. 'As soon as I've had a cuppa.'

Sheena took out another cup. Usually, Laurie dashed off to her dad's before the last plate was put away. Did she need to talk?

'So what's wrong?'

'I saw Des Turner on Friday. He's putting me forward for a job – a big job – a stately home in Lancashire.'

'So why the long face?'

'It's Kingsley Hall.'

Sheena was none the wiser.

'That's where Dad was–'

'Oh, my–! You mean–?'

'Yes.'

Sheena didn't know what to say. Laurie never talked about it, but Sheena knew Laurie's father had once worked as a butler, and had ended up in prison for a crime he didn't commit.

'The place has been empty for twenty years. Now Toby – it was his father who was killed–'

'Killed?'

Sheena supposed she shouldn't have been so shocked. She knew Laurie's dad had spent twelve years in prison, too long for stealing the family silver. She was shocked, though. Horrified.

'Toby plans to open the house and gardens to the public. It's a dream of a job, obviously, but – well, I don't know how Dad would feel about it, I don't know if Toby would even give me the job–' She groaned. 'I don't even know how I feel about it.'

In typical Laurie fashion, her face suddenly cleared.

'I need to talk to Dad before I do anything. I'll have a chat with him this afternoon.'

Sheena nodded, knowing better than to press for information.

'Sheena, do you think he'd recognise me? Toby, I mean? I was eight when he last saw me – he was thirteen.'

Looking at Laurie, Sheena had to smile.

'I don't know what you looked like as an eight-year-old, but I doubt you turned men's heads as you do now.

'Did you have a stunning figure in those days? Were you five feet ten, with gorgeous hair that would earn you a fortune if you went into shampoo advertising?'

Laurie had to laugh.

'I was tall – gawky, everyone said. And I had a brace on my teeth.' She thought for a moment. 'My hair was short in those days – mainly because I used to scream blue murder when anyone tried to brush it. I was a real tomboy. No, I'm sure he wouldn't recognise me.'

The frown returned.

'I've no idea how Dad will feel about it, though. He never talks about – you know.'

15

'His daughter doesn't, either,' Sheena pointed out, and saw surprise on Laurie's face.

Laurie was an extrovert, always the life and soul of the party, yet she never spoke of her past; Sheena had always supposed it was too painful.

'I'm sorry. It's just that there's nothing to be said. Dad was sent to prison – wrongly. Mum scrimped and saved to bring me up. Dad came home a changed man – and then–'

She shrugged, but Sheena knew Laurie's mum had died little more than a year after Jim Whitney came out of prison.

'You'd best go and see him, then. Give him my love, won't you?'

'Of course. And, Sheena – thanks.' She thought for a moment. 'I'm not being deliberately secretive, you know. It's just that I don't really know what happened. Mum wouldn't talk about it, and Dad won't.'

'Talk to your dad.'

Sheena knew Laurie better than she knew her own sister, and knew Laurie's dad – a kind, gentle man, who wouldn't hurt a living creature.

If Laurie said he was innocent of any crime, then that was good enough for Sheena. He wouldn't be the first man wrongly imprisoned...

'It's a cracking afternoon,' Jim Whitney declared. 'A bit chilly, but at least it's dry. Let's have a walk through the park, eh?'

'Good idea, Dad.'

Laurie knew Dad always wanted to walk in the fresh air. She knew why, too.

'You never know,' she added in a teasing voice, 'we might see Scooby Doo.'

'Ha, enough of that nonsense!'

Laurie laughed.

Scooby Doo was a Great Dane, but it was his owner who interested Laurie, a blonde, smartly-dressed woman in her mid-fifties. Pamela would always stop for a chat, ever since the day Scooby Doo had nearly knocked Laurie into the lake.

Laurie kept hoping her dad might show some interest, but it seemed a lost cause. Pamela, on the other hand, was definitely interested in him.

What might a stranger see when they looked at her dad? A slight, frail man, with a wiry frame and thinning dark hair, a man who held himself very erect, yet who looked older than his fifty-nine years.

Would they see the kind, gentle soul he was? Or spot the love in his eyes whenever he gazed at his daughter?

'This is more than a bit chilly, Dad!' There was a bitterly cold wind.

'We can't expect much better for March. Still, at least it's not raining.'

17

Laurie wasn't complaining. Like her dad, she preferred to be in the fresh air, which was partly why she'd loved horticultural college.

She'd wanted to go to university, like her friends, but there hadn't been the money for that, and gardening school had seemed the next best thing. She'd been able to get evening work in a local pub to help with the finances.

Now, though, she thanked her lucky stars she hadn't gone to university. She loved her work.

They linked arms as they walked, and caught up on each other's news.

'Let's sit on the bench for a bit,' she suggested after a while. 'I need to talk to you, Dad.'

'Problems?' he asked, concerned.

'Not really.' She wished Scooby Doo and his owner would appear; she really wasn't comfortable discussing this.

'Des Turner is putting my name forward for a job possibility,' she said, plunging in.

'Excellent. It was Des who got you the job at the hospice, wasn't it?'

'Yes, but the thing is – well, this job is designing the gardens at–' She swallowed, and the next words came out in a whisper. 'Kingsley Hall.'

Her dad stiffened, and when she looked at him, she saw how pale he'd gone.

She couldn't remember the last time that

place had been mentioned. Certainly not since Mum died, and that was six years ago.

Oh, Mum, I wish you were here now. We could do with your gentle commonsense...

'I told Des I was interested in this job before I knew where it was,' she said. 'I can easily give him a call and tell him to forget it.'

'I heard young Toby was back.' Dad's eyes were clouded with memories, none of them good, Laurie suspected.

'Really? How?'

'Folk tell me things.'

Laurie had no idea who he meant.

'According to Des, he wants to open up the place to the public.'

Her dad stared at the lake, saying nothing.

'Dad—' She slipped her arm through his. 'You've never really spoken about what happened that night. I wish you'd tell me about it.'

'It's a long time ago, love.'

'I know, but it's always – there.'

'Oh, yes. It's always there.' He sounded bitter, and Laurie wasn't surprised.

She waited, but he was still staring at the lake.

'What do I do?' she asked at last. 'Do I tell Des to forget it? Or do I go up there and talk to Toby about this job?'

'The choice is yours, Laurie.'

'But how can I go if it's going to upset you

19

so much?'

He patted her arm, and let out a long sigh.

'It was Guy Fawkes Night, 1985,' he said speaking with great reluctance. 'Just a normal Tuesday night. They'd had a party at the hall – a bonfire and fireworks – the Saturday before.' He smiled at her, but it was a tight smile.

'You loved that!'

'I vaguely remember it,' she told him, her throat dry. 'At least, I think I do – sometimes I don't know what I remember and what I've imagined.

'I remember the Hall, though, and I remember riding Toby's ponies, and I remember his father, too. He was kind to me. I remember him giving me apples from the orchard.'

'Do you really?' This time, Dad's smile came more easily. 'Aye, he was a good man. He loved the gardens, too, and that's how I came to be butler. Mr Edward would often chat to my dad – your granddad, who was gardener at the Hall.

'It was Mr Edward – Toby's dad – who decided I should have the post of butler, and sent me to be trained.

'Aye, he was a good man. How anyone could think–' He shook his head.

'Anyway, that night, Mr Edward had gone to bed, you and your mum were asleep, and I was tidying up downstairs. Before locking up for the night, I often used to step outside for a smoke. I did that night.'

He fell silent, and Laurie waited.

'When I'd finished my cigarette, I went back inside and locked up the back of the house. I then went, as I did every night, to check the safe in Mr Edward's study – he kept his late wife's jewellery in there; a beautiful amethyst and diamond necklace, bracelet and matching earrings.

'They were worth a few bob, no doubt about it, but it was the sentimental value behind them. She'd adored that jewellery – given to her by Mr Edward on their wedding day – and he often went to the safe to look at it. Many's the time I'd see him holding the necklace to the light, his eyes misty with memories.'

'How long had she been gone?' Laurie asked.

'Eight years – pneumonia. Mr Edward and Toby were devastated, as you might imagine. That family has known tragedy, no doubt about it.'

So has this one, Laurie thought.

'What happened when you went to the safe?' she prompted him.

'It was open,' he said grimly. 'The door was wide open, and it was empty except for a few worthless papers.'

Laurie held her breath.

'I headed for the stairs to tell Mr Edward,

but he must have heard the intruder and disturbed him, because he was lying on the stairs with a huge gash to the back of his head.'

Laurie gasped, and pulled her coat tighter.

'I was going to phone the police,' her dad went on, 'but then I could smell burning. Whoever had killed Mr Edward and stolen the jewellery intended the place to burn to the ground. You and your mum were asleep upstairs, and my only thought was to get you to safety.'

Laurie remembered standing on the lawn, clinging to her mum, watching the house burn. It wasn't a good memory. She'd been crying for her dad, she recalled, and her mum had been trying to soothe her.

'Did you phone the police and the fire brigade?' she asked quietly.

'Someone had beaten me to it,' he said, and the bitterness in his voice had Laurie shivering even more.

'Before I knew it,' he went on, 'I was being charged.'

'With what, though?' She'd never really understood.

'It came down to manslaughter.' His voice was so tight he could barely speak. 'According to the police, only me and Mr Edward knew how to open the safe. He was dead, so that left me. There was no sign of a break-in, and if Mr Edward had heard the intruder, they reckoned I would have, too.'

'They couldn't send you to prison for that, though, Dad. Surely!'

'No.' He paused for long moments. 'An envelope arrived for me the following morning. Inside was two thousand pounds. Cash.'

Laurie had never been told about that!

'I suppose you can't blame them for jumping to conclusions,' he said, although it was clear to Laurie that he did blame them.

'I had no idea about the cash,' she murmured.

'No, well, your mum reckoned it was wrong to talk about it all in front of you. It was hard for your mum, love. Very hard.'

Laurie nodded.

'I know, Dad.'

'Anyway, they reckoned I'd been bribed to steal the jewels, and must have killed Mr Edward when he caught me in the act.' He scowled at a couple of ducks. 'How could I have done that? The man was like family!'

'Oh, Dad.' Laurie hugged him tight.

'You do realise,' her dad said grimly, 'that Toby wouldn't allow you within a hundred miles of his property?'

'I know.' She hardly dared to breathe. Was he saying it was OK for her to go to Kingsley Hall?

'But my name's changed. Besides, he'd never recognise me. I was just a kid who used to be hanging around when he was home from boarding school.'

'Do you want to go?'

Laurie pulled back to look at him.

'I don't know,' she admitted. 'My feelings are mixed. It's a dream of a job, of course. But–'

'But what?'

'I'm torn,' she admitted, 'between letting the past go – as you always say we should–'

'I might say that,' he interrupted her, 'but I know how impossible it is. That night will haunt me to the grave.'

Laurie shuddered, and hugged him again.

'Between letting go of the past,' she carried on, 'or facing up to it. Sometimes, Dad, you have to face up to demons.'

'I know you do, love, but – oh, I'd be a liar if I said I haven't dreamed of finding out who set me up. And done my damnedest to find out. But now – well, where has it got me? Nowhere. I'm too old for any of that. It's over.'

A few spots of rain fell. They got to their feet and headed back. As they walked, everything became clear to Laurie. More than anything, she wanted to clear her dad's name. By going back to Kingsley Hall, she might just be able to do that...

When her dad had been arrested, Laurie and her mum had moved far away from Lancashire, and ended up in a small flat in Middlesex. They'd never gone back, but now, it was time.

'It'll do no harm to talk to Toby about this job,' she said firmly. 'I might not get it, but if I do, I'm going to accept it, Dad.'

'Don't get any ideas about digging into the past, love.'

She felt herself flush.

'You'll be wasting your time,' he told her. 'It's twenty years ago – folk will have forgotten.'

'I know.'

'No-one cares,' he said, but he was wrong about that. He cared. She cared, too…

When Laurie got home, she found Sheena chatting on the phone.

'It's that ex-husband of yours,' her flatmate said, smiling as she held out the phone.

'Thanks.' Laurie took it from her. 'Steve, hello! I was going to call you this evening.'

'Tsk. I should have waited and let you run up your phone bill!'

She laughed, and settled down for a chat.

'I wanted to talk to you about this job I'm going after,' she said.

Steve was a good listener. He was a good man, too. Yet again, she wondered what had gone wrong with their marriage.

The truth was, they'd married too young, when they'd had no idea what marriage entailed.

She'd been eighteen when they fell in love, just nineteen when they married. Almost from their wedding day, they seemed to drift further and further apart. Less than four years later, they'd divorced.

Oh, it was very amicable, but all the same…

'And how does Jim feel about you going to Kingsley Hall?' Steve asked.

'I've been talking to him about it this afternoon. You know Dad – he wants whatever I want.'

'Mm.'

'But for the first time ever, he actually spoke about what happened that night…'

Again, Steve listened without interrupting as she told him the whole story.

'That's a lot of circumstantial evidence, love,' he said when she'd finished.

'Steve, you don't think–?'

'No!'

Sudden tears stung her eyes. For a moment, she'd thought Steve had doubts about her dad. She should have known better.

'Laurie, of course I don't! How can you think so?'

'I know. I'm sorry.'

'I should think so.'

Steve's love was conservation. He was working in Scotland at the moment but, whenever he was home, he made straight for Laurie's dad. They spoke on the phone often, too. Her dad always reckoned Steve was the son he never had, and the feeling was mutual.

'Why exactly do you want this job so badly?'

'It's exactly the sort of job I've always wanted. The place is vast.'

'Nothing to do with your dad?'

'Of course not. I was excited before I even knew where it was.' Laurie crossed her fingers. That was nearly true.

'Hmm. Well, so long as you don't take off for Lancashire complete with deer stalker and magnifying glass!'

She had to laugh.

'I'm serious, Laurie. What good will raking up the past do?'

A lot – if she uncovered the truth. Realistically, though, she doubted if that were possible.

Her silence spoke volumes to Steve, who knew her so well.

'Let it go,' he said. 'Jim couldn't face going through that again.'

'He could if it proved his innocence!'

'But it won't, Laurie. They thought him guilty then, but by this time all the evidence has long gone. The people involved will have forgotten about it – or died.'

'I haven't even got the job yet,' she reminded him.

'Let me know what happens.'

'I will!'

Time to change the subject, Laurie

decided. He didn't approve of her wanting to try to clear Dad's name. At least, he thought it was a lost cause. Perhaps it was.

'So tell me all your news,' she suggested, and they chatted for another twenty minutes.

Laurie spent the weekend exploring the Lancashire-Yorkshire border and doing a lot of walking over the hills, but she remembered none of it. Even the Pennines, so bleak in the rain and wind of the weekend, had seemed foreign to her. Surprisingly beautiful, but foreign.

Now, though, it was Monday morning. Time to leave the hotel in Todmorden and drive to Kingsley Hall for her ten o'clock appointment with Toby Davis.

She'd forced herself to eat toast and cereal. She'd need the fuel today, but her nerves were in shreds.

What if Toby recognised her?

Of course he wouldn't. She scoffed at herself. Eight-year-old Laura Whitney bore no resemblance whatsoever to twenty-six-year-old Laurie Summerfield...

She drove through Bacup. Seven miles to go. Her heart was hammering and her throat painfully tight.

It was a dry morning, with a light mist on the surrounding hills. The sun might even break through later.

As she drove, she pictured the house. She could remember it well, although she guessed

28

it might look smaller now. It was a long stone building, with lots of windows on three floors. The stable block had been at the back, she recalled, and the kitchen had been huge, with two massive scrubbed pine tables in the centre.

Suddenly, there was no more time to think, because she was turning into the driveway. There was no gate, just a cottage by the side of the road.

The drive was flanked with trees. She didn't remember those, yet they'd clearly been alive a lot longer than she had.

She rounded a bend in the drive, and there it was. She slowed so abruptly that she stalled the engine. Cursing beneath her breath, she restarted, but didn't move.

She'd been wrong; the Hall looked bigger than she remembered. It was a long building with eight windows on the ground floor and ten on both the first and second floors. Imposing wasn't the word for it! My, it was grand.

The drive seemed to go on for ever, but eventually, it curved round to the left, and to the Hall porch.

In a sudden moment of panic, Laurie doubted her ability to get out of her car and walk to the door. And what a door it was – a massive oak thing with a bell pull at the side. She'd forgotten that.

As she watched, the door suddenly opened.

A man and a dog came down the steps. The man was wearing tight trousers and a jumper, and the dog's coat gleamed.

With a deep breath, Laurie got out of her car and walked towards them.

'Are you Laurie Summerfield, by any chance?'

'I – yes.'

It couldn't be. No, never in a million years!

'Toby Davis.' He would have shaken her hand, but his dog decided to greet Laurie by trying to lick her face.

'Holly!'

The dog very reluctantly stopped, and dropped to Toby's feet.

Laurie struggled to look him in the face. She couldn't remember him being tall, but now he had to be a good six inches taller than she was. He'd been dark-haired, of course, but his hair now was a deep brown.

And he'd been nothing to look at, or perhaps, at eight, she simply hadn't noticed such things. This Toby was tall, broad and very pleasing on the eye.

His accent was impossible to place. Not surprising, really, she supposed, given that he'd lived abroad for so long.

'Pleased to meet you,' she managed. 'Er – am I too early?'

She was only fifteen minutes early, but he looked as if he was going out somewhere.

'Not at all. I thought I'd walk along the

30

drive to meet you.' He looked her up and down.

'I expected someone older,' he said, and Laurie's heart sank. 'I like punctuality, though,' he added.

Toby will be late for his own funeral... The memory came from nowhere. She could remember his father saying that, laughter in his voice, as they'd waited for Toby to help load up the ponies for the local gymkhana...

The memory shook her. If she wanted this job, and she did, she would have to forget the past for the time being.

'I thought we'd walk the estate first,' Toby said briskly, 'before it rains. Then we can discuss my plans inside. Does that suit you, Miss Summerfield?'

'Yes, of course.'

Her memories were of a fun-loving young boy, looking forward to being spoilt during his school holidays. This was a businessman. She needed to ignore the sudden assault of memories and be businesslike, too.

'The orchard will have to go,' he was saying. 'In its place will be a small farm park and kids' play area.'

He must have spotted the look of horror on her face, for he smiled suddenly.

'I know, but apparently it brings the punters in.'

'Yes. I'm sure it does.'

'I also want to have something special in

the gardens – anyway, forget that for now. I've reams of plans back at the house. Just get to know the place.'

She didn't need to. Even the small island in the middle of the lake was familiar to her. A pair of swans used to nest there, she recalled. She could remember feeding the cygnets...

Laurie was soon breathless, not from exertion, but because her heart refused to do anything but race, and all the while Toby talked.

'I want to employ local people to do the actual work,' he said. 'I hope that's OK with you?'

'Of course.'

He was talking as if she already had the job, as if he thought she could provide exactly what he needed! In truth, her mind was a blank. She might never have designed a garden in her life.

Laurie pulled herself together.

'I gather you're working to a tight budget?' she said.

'Very. I'll show you the figures back at the house. Oh, and I warn you, Miss Summerfield, a lot of people reckon my plans aren't feasible.'

'And if they're not?'

He thought for a moment.

'I lose my home.'

She shivered.

'Has it been in your family a long time?'

'Since 1740.'

'And who lives here now?'

'Only me.'

He wasn't the chattiest of people!

'You've been abroad, I hear.'

'Yes.' He didn't elaborate, and they were soon back at the house. They'd been walking for almost three hours, and Laurie's stomach was protesting.

Perhaps he heard it.

'We'll have lunch,' he said, 'then I'll show you my plans.'

The house was exactly as Laurie remembered it – except it was very bare.

'I expected to see your ancestors gazing down from the staircase,' she said lightly. As they always had been…

'And so you shall.' Again, he didn't elaborate.

How many people, she wondered, had her dad opened the oak door to?

They ate in the kitchen – the two tables had been replaced by a much smaller one – and tucked into salad, cold meat and pies that someone had laid out for them.

'Did you make lunch?' she asked curiously.

'No.' The thought seemed to amuse him. 'I have the wonderful Mrs Mason to tend my needs. She used to live at the house, but–' He shrugged.

Mrs Mason must be a hundred! Heaven's

she'd been housekeeper when Laurie had lived there.

Would she recognise Laurie if their paths crossed?

'My father died when I was thirteen,' Toby said. 'I lived abroad with my aunt and uncle. He was in the diplomatic corps, so we travelled a lot. All the furniture was put in store. I've never been back until now.'

'I see.' *My father died.* 'It's a very beautiful part of the world.'

'Yes. Shall we take coffee into the study?' he asked.

'That would be nice. Thank you, Mr Davis.'

'Toby, please.'

'Laurie.'

'Short for Laura?'

'No! Er, no.'

She couldn't remember the study at all. Presumably it would have been out of bounds to Laurie as a child. Her dad would have been here often, though.

It was a lovely room, where you wanted to curl up in one of the leather armchairs with a good book, beside a crackling log fire.

The fire hadn't been lit. A pity; it wasn't too warm.

The comfy-looking leather armchairs were ignored. Toby sat on one side of the vast mahogany desk, and Laurie on the other. The dog, Holly, followed them in, decided they weren't going to do anything exciting, and promptly dropped down in front of the cold fireplace. A subtle hint, perhaps...

Laurie soon became so caught up in Toby's plans, and explaining her ideas to him, that she forgot the temperature.

'Personally, I'd keep the orchard and turn it into a kitchen garden. There would be the apple trees, of course, and you could have a riot of bulbs in spring. It's the perfect spot for an old-fashioned rose garden as well as the traditional fruit and vegetables.'

'But what about this confounded play area for the kids?'

Laurie had to smile.

'That could go to the side of the stable block – here.' She pointed at the spot in his plans. 'Plenty of room there for the climbing frames and stuff. And then the farm animals could go – here.

'The croquet lawn,' she went on, 'needs enclosing with tall hedges. Oh, and where the cedar trees are, you want azaleas and rhododendrons and–'

She stopped.

'Sorry, I'm getting carried away.'

'No, I like it. Carry on...'

On she went, seeing it all in her mind's eye.

Three hours passed.

'We haven't discussed your salary,' Toby said suddenly, 'or where you're to live. I'm so sorry – I got a bit carried away myself. I thought the cottage – the one at the end of the drive. Would you care to take a look?'

'Yes. Yes, I would.'

Minutes later, they were rattling down the drive in Toby's Land-Rover, with the dog breathing hotly down Laurie's neck.

'It hasn't been lived in for years,' Toby explained, 'but I've had it checked out and some furniture installed. It's very basic, I'm afraid.'

'I can do basic,' she assured him.

He stopped outside the cottage, and they climbed out.

'I need to make a call.' He took his mobile phone from his pocket. 'Have a look round and see what you think.'

The cottage was idyllic. Two bedrooms, kitchen, dining-room, sitting-room, enormous bathroom and – best of all – its own garden, complete with dilapidated summer-house.

'Will it be all right?' Toby asked when he caught up with her.

'It's perfect,' she told him. 'Does this mean – well, the job? Do you have other people to see?'

He looked surprised by the suggestion.

'Oh, no. No, I thought you – well, I'd very much like you to take on the work.'

A huge lump wedged itself in her throat, and tears stung at her eyes.

'Thank you.' Her voice must have sounded clipped; she was struggling to talk at all.

She had the strangest sensation of coming home.

Oh, she felt a little guilty. After all, Toby wouldn't allow her within sight of the house if he knew who she was or, more accurately, who her father was.

But Dad was innocent, and that lessened the guilt. And come hell or high water, she was going to prove it to the world.

'It's funny,' Toby broke into her thoughts, 'but I keep getting the feeling I've seen you before.'

A chill ran down Laurie's back.

'Really?' She gave a tinkling little laugh. 'I can't imagine where...'

Unable to look at him, she turned her gaze towards the house.

Kingsley Hall seemed to be welcoming her home. If only those old walls could talk ... then the truth would come out.

But she was here. She'd got the job. She had begun.

CHAPTER TWO

'If this doesn't work out, you can always open a bookshop,' Sheena quipped, and Laurie laughed. 'I've overdone it, haven't I?'

She'd tried not to bring much to her new

home, because the cottage was already well furnished. But it had taken hours to sort out the books she couldn't possibly live without, and the pile seemed to have grown.

'I'll have a good clear out one of these days,' she vowed.

'I've heard that one before!' Stepping over boxes waiting to be unpacked, Sheena walked to the window. 'It's a lovely place, though. I'm envious.'

'It is, and I feel at home already.' The doubts she'd been trying to ignore suddenly hit her.

'I just hope I'm not out on my ear within the week! My nerves will be in shreds waiting for Toby to recognise me.'

'He won't,' Sheena said confidently. 'Those old photos your dad showed me – no-one would recognise you.'

'I hope you're right.' Laurie pushed her worries aside. 'Come on, let's wander down to the pub. My treat – a thank-you for coming up for the weekend.'

'You know I wouldn't have missed it for the world. But, as you're offering...'

Steve had offered to drive down from Scotland to help Laurie move in, but she hadn't wanted people to know she was divorced. Silly, perhaps, but if anyone discovered her maiden name was Whitney...

Anyway, it wasn't that she needed help with the actual unpacking; more that she wanted moral support.

The rain was holding off, so they walked the half-mile into the village.

Years ago, the whole of Kingsley had belonged to the estate. These days, it was a thriving village that boasted an impressive range of shops, a twice-weekly market, and no fewer than five pubs. And Toby Davis owned very little of it.

The pub they made for was the Farrars' Arms, with the promise of home-cooked food served all day. They were soon settled in a corner, as close to the log fire as they could get, tucking in to steak and ale pie.

Three elderly gentlemen were sitting at the bar, putting the world happily to rights.

'I bet they've lived here all their lives,' Laurie said quietly. 'And I bet they remember what happened at the Hall that night.'

'They'll remember what they were told happened,' Sheena corrected her. 'And no doubt the stories have been exaggerated over the years. What exactly was stolen that night, Laurie?'

'Apparently, Toby's dad kept his late wife's jewellery in the safe – must have been worth a few bob. I'm going to pay a visit to the library,' Laurie told her friend. 'One of the local libraries is sure to have old newspapers on file.'

Sheena winced.

'It'll make for pretty depressing reading,

love, with your dad the villain of the piece.'

'I know that.'

Her dad was innocent, though, so it would be all right.

But, as Sheena had been good enough to give up her weekend to help her move in, Laurie wasn't going to depress her.

'So what do you think of my new home?'

'I love it. I love your cottage, this village, the countryside, the hills – everything. It will be gorgeous in the summer.'

'Do you think summer comes this far north?' Laurie asked, and Sheena laughed.

'Probably not. It's certainly a bit cold – considering it's the middle of April, spring doesn't look like putting in an appearance.'

'I gather all the hikers descend on the place – walking the Pennine Way, and suchlike.'

'Rather them than me – these hills are seriously big...'

Instead of heading straight back to the cottage, they decided to walk round the village. It was outside the bank that all Laurie's worries came rushing back. Walking briskly down the steps was Toby Davis.

It was too late to pretend they hadn't seen him. And after all, from Monday, Laurie would be working for him. She could easily expect to see him most days.

'Laurie, hello!' He shook her hand vigorously, which she thought a little over the top.

'Hello, er, Toby.' She gave him a bright smile and introduced him to Sheena. 'She's travelled up for the weekend to help me move in.'

'Splendid! Pleased to meet you, Sheena.' Her hand was shaken just as vigorously.

'Is everything all right at the cottage? I planned to call in this afternoon to make sure you had everything you needed. I asked Mrs Mason to stock up your cupboards – did she manage that?'

'She did, thank you.' Laurie felt guilty now that they'd had lunch out.

Mrs Mason, who according to Dad was only in her mid-sixties, despite Laurie reckoning she must be closer to a hundred, had done them proud. The fridge had been stocked with milk, eggs, bacon and tomatoes, and the cupboards were full.

'It was very kind of you – her,' she added.

'And everything else is all right?' Toby asked.

'It's fine, thank you.'

He nodded, then seemed at a loss.

'Well, you have my number if there's anything you need, Laurie.'

'Yes. Thank you.'

He nodded again.

'Good to meet you, Sheena, and I'll see you on Monday, Laurie, if our paths don't cross before.'

He strode away and Laurie was aware that

she'd been holding her breath.

If he hadn't recognised her by now, and there was no reason he should, he was unlikely to. She had to calm down.

'Well, I never,' Sheena breathed. 'You said he "wasn't bad looking"!'

'He isn't. Not everyone's type, perhaps, but not bad.'

'Not bad?' Sheena rolled her eyes. 'Laurie, you need an eye test. The man is gorgeous. Absolutely gorgeous. And so nice with it. Polite, caring, charming, attractive, rich – he's the perfect man.'

'He wouldn't be if he knew who I was,' Laurie murmured, biting her bottom lip. 'And anyway, he's not rich. He's broke, which is why he's having to open the Hall to the public.'

'Oh, tish,' Sheena scoffed. 'There's broke, and then there's broke. I wouldn't mind being that kind of broke. How much would the Hall fetch if he put it on the market? Enough to keep me in luxury for a good few years!'

'I suppose so,' Laurie agreed.

They carried on walking.

'Strange to think you used to spend the school holidays with him,' Sheena mused.

'I always thought him a bit spoilt in those days,' Laurie told her. 'Though I missed him when he went back to boarding school. Living so far out of the village, I suppose I was short of company. I would have missed anyone.'

'Well, I think he's wonderful. Fancy getting his housekeeper to stock up the cottage! How thoughtful!'

'It was,' Laurie agreed.

'Do you remember this Mrs Mason?'

'Yes.'

Sally Mason had been kindness herself, Laurie recalled, often putting hot, freshly-made biscuits into a little girl's eager hand…

'It was all a long time ago. They were happy days, for Mum and Dad, as well as for me, but now – well, my family's name is–' She shrugged.

'Come on, let's go and unpack those boxes,' Sheena slipped an arm through hers.

'In case I'm fired on Monday, and need to open a bookshop?'

'Pessimist!' Sheena laughed. 'You'll be fine.'

Thursday was late-night opening at the library, so Laurie had booked the microfiche machine for an hour.

The room was quiet, and Laurie was glad of an excuse to sit down for an hour. She'd walked miles on the estate over the last few days. Then, in the evenings, she'd been busy getting the cottage organised to her liking.

Having been shown how to use the machine, she quickly sped through the pages. Because she hadn't wanted to arouse suspicion, she'd asked to see the newspapers from the Eighties. There was a lot to get through before she reached that fateful night of November 5, 1985.

It was all too easy to get distracted too. The news seemed to be from a different age. How the world had changed!

Here it was – November, 1985.

There was a write-up about the bonfire party held at the Hall the previous Saturday. A photograph showed the Hall against a backdrop of fireworks, another showed Toby's dad, Mr Edward, smiling broadly for the camera, and a final one showed the crowd enjoying the spectacle.

Laurie thought she might have been in the final photograph, but she couldn't recognise herself.

Heart hammering, she leafed on, and then the headline hit her: *Murder At Kingsley Hall.*

Laurie shuddered, despite the warmth of the library.

A formal photograph of Mr Edward took up most of the front page. The story told how he'd disturbed a burglar in the early hours of the morning, and had been murdered while trying to save his late wife's jewels.

There were long paragraphs extolling his virtues, and quotes from several local people saying how shocked they were, and how the village would never be the same.

Turning to the next page, Laurie saw two

smaller photographs, one of a young Toby, and another of his mother.

There was no mention of the jewels, and the fire received only a passing mention. The fire service's quick response had undoubtedly saved the Hall from ruin, it said.

She moved on again.

Butler questioned by police. The headline screamed at her, and Laurie felt tears spring to her eyes.

She blinked them back, irritated with herself. What had she expected? Her dad had been convicted...

There was a photograph of Dad, which took her completely by surprise. He looked so young! Young, fit and healthy.

On a separate page, there were photographs of the jewellery that had once belonged to Toby's mother. The report was written in a way that made it impossible to know for sure which pieces had been stolen. Perhaps the reporter hadn't known.

The largest photograph showed a necklace, and the accompanying description made Laurie gasp.

The Kingsley Diamond. No value was given, but it had to be worth an absolute fortune. The necklace itself was studded with sixty diamonds and a large diamond, described as violet-coloured, hung down like a teardrop.

People might have recognised the Kingsley Diamond itself, but broken down into pieces, Laurie assumed it would have been easy enough for any thief to sell...

A dark shadow fell across the screen, and she swung round, to find herself looking into Toby's face.

She was so shocked that she almost screamed.

He stared at the screen, and then at her. Laurie vaguely wondered if either of them would ever find the power of speech again, but then he spoke, his voice gruff and none too even.

'The butler did it.'

Laurie swallowed.

'Sorry,' he said, pulling himself together. 'I didn't mean to startle you.' He nodded at the papers in his hand.

'I've come to get more photocopies of these plans. The machine here does the large copies.'

'Ah, I see.' Her face was burning now. She'd been well and truly caught out.

'Have you eaten?' he asked suddenly.

'Eaten?' She was so surprised by the question, and still trying to recover from his sudden, startling appearance, that she couldn't remember.

'There's an Italian place round the corner,' he said. 'I thought I'd have a bite to eat there, and I'd be happy if you joined me.'

'Oh, er, right.' She didn't have the nerve to

refuse. 'Yes, thank you, that sounds good.'

It sounded like her worst nightmare come true!

'Shall we meet there in, say, half an hour?'

'Yes, lovely.'

He nodded, then walked through the archive room into the room next door. Laurie soon heard the photocopier in action…

She turned back to the screen, but the words danced before her eyes, making no sense whatsoever.

How on earth was she going to eat anything? What would she say? What would he say?

The butler did it. Oh, my…

But the butler *didn't* do it, she thought, sense slowly returning. She had to stop creeping around feeling guilty every time she laid eyes on Toby! This was not her fault. Her dad was innocent. He would have died for Mr Edward.

In half an hour, she was going to have to come up with an explanation as to why she'd been snooping into Toby's past…

She switched off the machine, and signed herself out.

The next ten minutes were spent in the Ladies'. She splashed cold water on her face, repaired her make-up, brushed her hair and walked, very, very slowly, out of the building to the Italian restaurant.

She'd hoped it might be full, but no such

luck, this being Thursday evening.

However, with a white wine in front of her, she was feeling slightly more composed when Toby joined her.

Once they'd ordered, Laurie took a deep breath.

'I'd had a thought,' she said briskly, 'which was why I was in the library. People like souvenirs of their days out, so I thought it might be a good idea to have a book written detailing the history of the Hall.'

'Mm,' he said.

'I thought perhaps I might find stories of ghosts – surely the Hall is haunted.'

'It's supposed to be.' He picked up his napkin and folded it in half. 'Actually, that's not a bad idea. There's a lot of history there, and I have loads of old documents.'

'What's this about a ghost, then?' she asked, beginning to relax a little.

Taking her completely by surprise, he laughed.

'You won't believe me if I tell you.'

'Try me.'

'Back in the early 1800s, a young maid fell in love with a visitor to the Hall. She was pregnant, sent word to him, and waited for him to return to the Hall to rescue her. When he didn't come back, she killed herself.'

Laurie gasped.

'On dark, winter nights, the sound of a horse's hooves can be heard racing away

48

from the Hall. Once they've died away, the young maid is seen at the window, moaning for her lost love.'

Laurie rubbed her arms to try to get rid of the goosebumps.

'Have you heard the horse? Seen the maid?'

'No.' His expression said he didn't believe such nonsense. 'Others claim they have, though. I expect it's nothing more than the wind in the trees.'

'That wouldn't explain the young girl at the window,' she pointed out.

'True enough.'

'It would make for interesting reading.'

She wanted to ask about the Hall's more recent history, about the Kingsley Diamond – oh, she had a million questions for him.

But she was too shaken to bring up any of them now. They would have to wait. There was no point pushing her luck.

On Monday night, as he did every Monday, Jim Whitney sat at his friend Micky's kitchen table and dealt a hand of cards.

This evening, though, his mind was miles away. It was just as well they only played for matches!

'How's that daughter of yours settling in at Kingsley Hall?' Micky asked, and Jim's head flew up.

'Well, there's obviously something bothering you,' Micky said knowingly, 'and I can only imagine it's young Laurie.'

Micky Reagan had proved a good friend to Jim, one of the best. They'd shared a cell and much more than that, their problems, their hopes and dreams.

When Jim had walked free, he'd vowed to put the past behind him, but he couldn't have coped without Micky's friendship.

Micky had served four years. A hit-and-run driver had killed one of his friends, and Micky, typically, had taken the law into his own hands...

'I don't like her being there,' Jim told him. 'At first, I wasn't too worried, but – oh, you know what she's like. She's a great one for delving into stuff that's best forgotten. Like a terrier with a bone, she is.'

'That's Laurie.' Micky smiled fondly, and got to his feet.

'I'll put the kettle on.'

'Just look at us,' Jim said, scowling. 'Two hardened criminals – gambling for matches, and drinking tea!'

'Do you want a beer?'

Jim shook his head.

'No, thanks.'

The card game was forgotten, the matches pushed aside, and they sat drinking tea and munching absently on biscuits.

'I wonder where she gets it from,' Micky mused. 'Laurie, I mean. A terrier with a bone. Who else fits that description?'

For the first time that evening, Jim actually smiled.

'Aye, she's a chip off the old block all right.' He spoke with pride.

'I can see her point, though,' Micky went on. 'Let's face it, you've been thinking about that night for nigh on twenty years. The puzzle is relatively new to young Laurie. Like you, she'll want it solved.'

'But that's the point – it'll never be solved now.'

Micky didn't argue with that.

'I keep going over and over it.' Jim didn't usually take sugar in his tea, but he stirred it anyway. 'Someone obviously knew the combination to that safe, and the more I think about it the more I come to realise how easy it would have been for anyone to get hold of it.'

'How's that?'

'Mr Edward had a habit of showing those jewels to anyone who displayed the slightest interest,' Jim explained. 'He did quite a bit of entertaining, and he'd often go and open the safe to show someone the contents. All that person had to do was stand behind him as he opened it.'

'What sort of folk did he entertain?'

'Not the likes of you and me,' Jim replied. 'Imagine someone in young Toby's position, say – someone strapped for cash, fighting to keep the family home. If that person were less than honest, he might resort to theft. He'd know the jewellery was insured so–' He shrugged.

'Steal a few jewels, get them broken down, sell them – where's the harm? Then down comes Mr Edward, catches him in the act, he panics, hits him over the head – and the next thing, theft has gone to murder.'

Micky pulled a face.

'You reckon that's what happened?'

'Twenty years on, and I still don't know what to think. Mr Edward wasn't entertaining that night and there was no sign of an intruder.'

'So what brought your Mr Edward down the stairs? He must have heard something.'

'Exactly!'

'Or – perhaps he didn't,' Micky went on. 'Perhaps he couldn't sleep – came downstairs for a drink or something, and had the shock of his life?'

They both mulled it over, as they'd done many times in the past.

'What's always stuck in my mind was that chap who called earlier on, reckoning he had an appointment with Mr Edward.'

'The fine arts chap?' Micky asked, and Jim nodded.

'That was queer, no doubt about it.'

Jim could still picture the stranger – tall, well-built, dark-rimmed glasses, wearing a suit that was a little too small for him. He hadn't looked like a successful dealer in fine arts. He'd looked too scruffy.

He'd called at the Hall one afternoon in October, when Mr Edward had been on holiday in Scotland, and insisted he had an appointment at three o'clock that afternoon. Jim had explained Mr Edward was away, and he'd assumed, knowing his boss could be a bit absent minded at times, that he had forgotten all about it.

This man, Charles Taylor, had said he'd seen Mr Edward a few weeks previously and had received a phone call saying he was considering selling some paintings.

That had been news to Jim, but there was no reason why Mr Edward would discuss the matter with him.

Before Charles Taylor left, he gave Jim his business card, and on Mr Edward's return, Jim had told him about the 'missed appointment'.

Mr Edward had never heard of the man, nor did he have any intention of selling any paintings.

'What did the police reckon?' Micky asked.

'Like everything else I said, they thought I was making it up to try to save my own skin,' Jim muttered. 'I didn't have the card to show them, more's the pity, but I remembered the chap's name and most of his address.'

'Which were false.' Micky nodded. 'So he

could have been weighing up the place?'

'Yes, but he couldn't have opened the safe.' As always Jim's thoughts brought him to a dead end.

'He could have forced Mr Edward to open it,' Micky pointed out.

'Aye, and that's another funny thing,' Jim said. 'The police are sure that Mr Edward was coming down the stairs when he was hit on the back of the head. That means our culprit must have gone up the stairs and got behind him!' He shook his head.

'It never has made sense, Micky, and I don't reckon it ever will!'

'Sounds like an inside job to me,' Micky said. 'Who was staying at the Hall that night?'

'Mr Edward. Young Toby was away at boarding-school, and Anne and Laurie were asleep upstairs. Normally, Sally Mason, the housekeeper, would have been there, but her sister had been taken ill and she'd dashed off to Carlisle. I was outside having a smoke. And that's your lot. There was no-one else there. Something else, too,' he went on. 'No-one ever knew who phoned the police and fire brigade. A man called 999, said the Hall was burning down and hung up. The police couldn't trace the call.'

There was no point going over it again.

'Come on,' he said, 'let's play cards.'

They played for an hour or so, but Jim's heart wasn't in it.

'So what's really bothering you?' Micky asked quietly. 'Are you worried about Laurie?'

Jim couldn't lie to his friend.

'Yes, I am. Someone out there knows exactly what happened that night, and if I get my hands on him–' He broke off. 'But whoever that person is, he isn't going to take kindly to some young girl digging it all up again. And he's already killed once.'

'Jim!' Micky was appalled. 'Hey, come on, mate. It's unlikely he meant to kill your Mr Edward. I expect he was as horrified as everyone else when he learned the man had died.'

Perhaps Jim was overreacting, but the more he thought about that night – and ever since Laurie had dropped her bombshell, he'd thought of nothing else – the more he worried.

'He could be dead by now,' Micky pointed out, 'but more likely, he's living the life of Riley on his riches – probably in the sunshine, abroad.'

Jim knew his friend was right. He was letting his imagination run away with him.

That was what happened, when your life was turned upside down and you ended up in a prison cell. They said it couldn't happen, not in this country. It only happened in books and films, and even then, it wasn't long before the truth came out. It certainly didn't happen to folk like him.

Yet it had happened, and as a consequence, Jim had lost faith in everything…

'Thanks, Micky.'

'For what?'

'Oh, for listening, for putting things in perspective.'

On Friday evening, after a long, tiring day, Laurie got back to her cottage, switched on the kettle for a much-needed cup of tea, and threw herself down in a chair.

She'd had a good day, though. They'd been working on the old maze which, after twenty years of neglect, was more of a jungle. It would have to be completely re-done, but she and Dave, head of her band of workers, had managed to trace the original design.

In her mind's eye, she could picture it – immaculate grass, neatly trimmed hedges, tall urns filled with irises or lilies at each corner…

A tap on her door disturbed her, and she was surprised to see Mrs Mason standing there, a box of eggs in her hand.

'Thought I'd drop these in for you, dear.'

'Oh, that's kind. Thank you. Will you come in? I've just put the kettle on.'

'Don't mind if I do,' Mrs Mason said, already through the door.

Laurie had to smile to herself. Mrs Mason had a heart of gold, but she had an incurable case of nosiness.

While Laurie made the tea, she saw, out of the corner of her eye, Mrs Mason running her finger along the dresser. Checking for dust? Fortunately Laurie had flicked round with a duster early that morning.

'You've got it lovely,' Mrs Mason said approvingly.

'It's a beautiful cottage,' Laurie said. 'I love everything about it. Let's sit outside, shall we?'

Over tea on the garden bench, the questions came thick and fast.

How did Laurie like Lancashire? Had she ever visited the county before? What plans did she have for the gardens? What did she think of Mr Toby? Did she think he'd ever get that daft dog trained?

Laurie leapt in with a few questions of her own.

'Have you worked here long, Mrs Mason?'

'Oh, call me Sally – everyone does. And yes, you could say that.' Her eyes crinkled at the edges. 'I've been here forty-eight years.'

She laughed at the surprise on Laurie's face.

'I started as a maid when I was sixteen,' she explained. 'There's not much I don't know about Kingsley Hall.'

'You must have seen some changes,' Laurie said lightly.

'Changes? You'd never believe it, dear!'

'I gather Toby has been abroad for years – it must be strange having him back?'

'It's marvellous.' Sally was beaming. 'Thirteen, he was, when his dad were killed.'

'Ah, yes, that was a dreadful thing,' Laurie murmured. 'I was in the library, seeing what I could find out about the original gardens here, and I read about that. Dreadful!'

'That it was. Why, it's nearly twenty years ago now, yet I still can't fully accept it.' She took a sip of her tea. 'Mind, it was a terrible time all round, what with that young man and everything.'

'Young man?'

'Oh, yes. The young curate. He'd only been in the village a year or so – in his mid-twenties, he was.'

Laurie waited for more, but for once, Sally Mason was silent.

'What happened to him?' Laurie asked curiously.

'Hmm?' Sally came to with a jolt. 'Vanished. Just like that.' She clicked her fingers. 'No trace of the poor chap. He's never been seen or heard of since.'

'How dreadful!'

'Nothing happened in Kingsley for years – well, nothing of importance,' Sally said, 'and then, within two months, we have that young lad missing and poor Mr Edward – dead.'

Laurie's mind was racing. How coincidental was that? Perhaps this curate had done a vanishing act, hidden locally, decided to steal some jewellery and then...

Who would suspect a curate?

Funny her dad had never mentioned this. She'd have to ask him what he could remember.

Sally Mason was looking at her quizzically.

'Is something wrong?' Laurie asked.

'Wrong? Good heavens, no. No, it's just that you put me in mind of someone, dear, and for the life of me, I can't think who it is.'

'How strange!' Laurie struggled to keep her voice light and level. 'Toby said I reminded him of someone, too. It must be one of his friends, I suppose.'

'That'll be it, I expect,' Sally agreed.

Laurie dared to breathe again. As Sheena had said, no-one would recognise her now. Perhaps she did look like one of Toby's friends...

'Now, where was I?' Sally murmured. 'Oh, the curate, yes. That shook the village, I can tell you. Everyone liked him.' Her voice dropped to a whisper.

'Between you and me, that's more than I can say about the vicar. No-one really took to Mr Casper – his sermons were more like rants, and a lot of folk took offence. To be fair, though, he was good at visiting folk. If you were ill, he'd soon be seeing if there was anything you needed, driving your relatives to visit you in hospital.

'In any case,' she went on, 'he didn't stay long. Kingsley had three vicars in three years – very unsettling, it was. Still, then we got Jacob Cunningham, and he's been here ever since. Lovely man, he is.'

'What a terrible time it must have been,' Laurie said, trying to get Sally's mind back on the past. 'And then poor Toby's father.'

'Oh, dreadful. Everyone loved Mr Edward. Everyone! When I think of that–'

Sally's voice dropped abruptly, and she stared at Laurie as if she'd seen a ghost.

'Oh, my!' she gasped. 'Little Laura Whitney!'

CHAPTER THREE

Had Sally Mason recognised Laurie? Or was she simply remarking on the strange resemblance?

'Little Laura Whitney, as I live and breathe,' Sally said.

'Is she a local girl?' Laurie asked innocently.

'Lovely young thing, she was.' Sally seemed to pull herself together. 'Daughter of Jim and Anne – Jim was butler here – it was him who murdered poor Mr Edward.'

'I didn't realise he'd had children,'

Laurie's voice said, apparently all by itself.

'Just the one. A lovely young thing, into everything, mind. She used to ride young Toby's ponies when he was at boarding school. A better rider than him, too – had a natural flair, if you know what I mean.'

Laurie hadn't so much as sat on a pony or a horse since the day she'd left here. There had been no money for such things.

'How long had the butler worked here?'

'It must have been twenty years. Like family, he was – we all were. And to think of him–' She shook her head.

'Twenty years? That's a long time.' Laurie had herself under control by now.

'Let me think.' Sally took a swallow of tea. 'His dad were gardener at the hall, but he wanted something better for his lad. It was Mr Edward who sent Jim off to college – a proper college for butlers, can you imagine that?'

Laurie shook her head.

'I reckon he started here around 1967. He married Anne in 1972, that I do remember. Oh, everyone was that happy! Little Laura, she'd have been born four or five years later – heavens, she'd be around your age now. The fourth of July she was born,' she added, astounding Laurie with her memory. 'And a right independent madam, too! Anyway, if Jim Whitney started work in '67, and the fire was in '85 – well, that's eighteen years.'

'That's odd, don't you think?' Laurie murmured. 'To work here for so long, and then suddenly do a dreadful thing like that?'

'Even now, I still can't believe it,' Sally said. 'The three of them seemed so happy – Jim, his wife, and little Laura. They never seemed to want for anything but each other. But there,' she added, stiffening, 'the taste of money does wicked things to folk.'

'Apparently,' Laurie murmured.

'He'll be out of prison now,' Sally mused. 'I wonder where he is? Living it up abroad, I shouldn't wonder.'

Laurie thought of her dad's small flat; his long hours working at the hotel; walking through the park, rain or shine, because he'd spent too long deprived of freedom and fresh air...

'From what you say, Sally, they don't seem the sort of family to live it up.'

'Appearances can be deceptive. We all found that out.'

Toby was standing in the hall, right next to the grandfather clock, when it suddenly struck, startling him. Nine o'clock.

'Master Toby!' Sally's voice carried well. 'If you don't get this dog out of my kitchen–'

Toby headed for the kitchen.

He's spent the last ten minutes looking for the wretched creature, but he should have

62

known. If Holly wasn't leaping over complete strangers and showering them with love in the form of sharp nips, she was in the kitchen trying to trip up his housekeeper, so that any food Sally might be carrying fell to the floor.

'I'll skin him, and you'll find yourself eating him for supper!' Sally declared.

'He's a she,' Toby corrected her. 'It's Holly. Quite right. I'll take her out.'

There was little point in expecting Holly to leave the tempting smells of the kitchen willingly. Toby hurried things along, dragging her from the room by her collar.

He left the house, buttoning his coat against the stiff wind, and stood for a moment on the steps as he tried to visualise Laurie Summerfield's gorgeous plans brought to life.

Ahead of him would be the circular, sunken rose garden. This, with the classical fountain in the centre, was likely to be his favourite place. The roses, Laurie had promised, would be interplanted with silver and mauve. Rustic seats would be positioned in the centre, and from there, it would be possible to admire the fine lines of the house or look south, along what would be the main walk.

This would lead down to the lake, and would comprise double herbaceous borders against formal beech hedges.

In the distance, by the lake, he could see

the woman herself. At least, he assumed it was Laurie – from this distance, it was difficult to tell.

Holly gave a short bark, then set off at a gallop.

'Holly! Confounded dog–'

Toby whistled but, if Holly heard, she paid him no heed. He set off in her wake.

The dog was making straight for Laurie.

'Sorry about that,' he said when he finally reached her. 'Holly's a bit–'

'She's fine.' Laurie was patting the dog, who had calmed down slightly. 'I enjoy her company, and all this racing around wears her out.'

'It wears *me* out,' Toby corrected her, and she laughed.

'You look a little lost,' he commented.

Until Holly had almost knocked her over, she'd been standing in one spot, staring up towards the house.

'Everything all right?' he added.

'Oh, yes, fine,' she said immediately. 'Dave and the gang should be up by the stable block – the digger's arriving this morning to level what will be the children's play area. I was on my way there, but I got stuck here, thinking about the herbaceous borders, or, more accurately the planting scheme. Obviously, we need something that will be of interest every season, but it's the colour and form – and the height, of course – I need to think about. With borders this long, they could easily become monotonous. We need to make sure they're at their best from June to September.' She warmed to her theme. 'But we want them to be interesting in winter, too, don't you agree?'

'I certainly do. When we last discussed this, you mentioned making the most of coloured foliage in the winter months.'

'Yes.' She nodded. 'I have a stack of photographs to show you – when you've half an hour to spare, I'll bring them over to the house and we'll decide what will look best.'

'Fine,' he said. 'Let me know when.'

Just then, they heard, and then saw, a huge yellow digger arriving.

'I'd better go and make sure they know what they're doing,' Laurie said, turning. 'Are you coming?'

'Why not?'

They strode along what would soon be the main walk towards the house, with Holly racing ahead, chasing leaves.

'By the way,' Laurie said suddenly, 'you said I reminded you of someone – I think I know who that someone is.'

There was something odd in her voice, something he couldn't quite define. She wasn't looking at him as she spoke, either, which in itself was strange. Usually, she was very direct in her dealings with him.

'Oh?'

'Yes, I was talking to Sally Mason and she said I reminded her of – oh, what was her name? – Lucy? Linda? – the former butler's daughter.'

He couldn't have been more surprised.

'Laura Whitney?' He had to laugh, despite the memories. 'No! Heavens, she was a scrawny thing – all teeth and legs, if I remember correctly.'

He thought for a moment, remembering those long ago days, something he usually avoided at all costs.

Laura had been a cheeky young tomboy with a brace on her teeth. He remembered her boxing his ears when he'd laughed at her. He would have boxed hers right back if his father hadn't appeared...

He couldn't imagine what Sally was thinking of! Laurie couldn't be more different from that gangling girl. Laurie was tall, slim and very attractive, poised and self-assured – elegant...

The choice of word made him smile. It took a very special woman to appear elegant when clad in jeans and wellington boots, and, more often than not, with her hair plastered to her face by the rain...

'Perhaps Sally got confused,' she said with a shrug. 'She was talking about the Whitney family – wondering where they might be now; living it up abroad somewhere, she thought.'

There was still a strange edge to her voice.

'I doubt it,' Toby said. 'There wasn't enough stolen to finance a high life.'

At last, she was looking directly at him, surprise all over her face.

'Not enough? But that old newspaper said the Kingsley Diamond was worth a fortune!'

'Not a fortune, exactly.' Enough, though, if the worst came to the worst and he had to sell it to hold on to Kingsley Hall. 'But the Diamond wasn't stolen.'

She frowned at him, puzzled.

'My father occasionally kept it with him and the necklace was in his bedroom that night.'

'And–' She cleared her throat. 'The butler didn't know that? You would have thought a man so trusted would have been aware of that, wouldn't you?'

'Apparently not,' Toby replied.

'How strange,' she murmured absently.

'Not really. The Kingsley Diamond would have been difficult to sell. Jim Whitney was an amateur. I expect he was satisfied with what he did steal.'

There was a pause.

'And that was?'

'A diamond necklace with matching bracelet and earrings – oh, various bits of jewellery.'

He could list them all, his mother's favourites, but they would have been broken up and sold long ago, and he preferred not to dwell on it.

Every time he thought about the way Whitney had deceived them all, it made him sick. To steal from the hand that fed, housed and clothed him and his family was bad enough, but...

Toby had been thirteen at the time. Along with his friends at school, he'd been looking forward to going home for the Christmas holidays.

He hadn't gone home that Christmas, or any other after that.

The headmaster had called Toby into his study to break the news and Toby's world had never been the same again.

He could still remember standing there, his head reeling, his world falling apart, struggling to keep every emotion at bay...

His father had visited the school only ten days earlier. He'd taken Toby out for tea and they'd walked round the town, talking about everything and nothing, laughing.

Now Dad was dead. He'd never see him again.

Even now, he struggled to believe it...

He looked up, surprised to see Laurie watching him, and tried to lighten the mood.

'The Kingsley Diamond is safe at the bank. If the worst comes to the worst, I'll be able to sell that to pay you!'

'It was your mother's, wasn't it?' she asked quietly.

'Yes. It would be difficult to part with, but not as difficult as parting with the Hall.'

He was relieved when they caught up with Dave Meredith and his workers.

Amazing to think that, in a very short time, this whole area behind the stable block would be flattened. Instead of ponies grazing in the field – not that ponies had, for twenty years – it would be home to hordes of children leaping around climbing frames. It wasn't a pleasant thought.

Still, hordes of children meant an income for the Hall…

'When they've finished here,' Laurie said, still a bit distracted, 'it'll be time to start on the rose garden.' She nodded to the spot in front of the house.

'That will be tricky, but I'll be glad when it's done – it'll be nice to get rid of that old path.'

She gazed around with a look of satisfaction.

'It'll be nice to get the main walk dug out and then we can move on down to the lake. There's not much to be done there – the main job is putting the fountain on the island.'

As always, the more Laurie talked about the gardens, the more excited Toby became. He'd been against opening the house and grounds to the public at first, and if he'd been able to think of a feasible alternative, he wouldn't have considered it. But now he was beginning to warm to the idea.

He loved Kingsley Hall passionately and, with Laurie's help, it was going to be restored to its original glory. It would be good to show it off. He'd worry about the finances later...

His enthusiasm was mainly due to Laurie. Her excitement was infectious, and her ideas were exactly what he wanted. Uncanny, really.

Toby wasn't a great believer in fate, but each day he thanked his lucky stars he'd found her. Could anyone else think along identical lines, when it came to the garden?

He'd been born at the hall and had loved it ever since, yet she'd never seen the place until recently. How could she love it so much? How could she think like he did?

After all, they were from completely different worlds.

Or were they? How did he know? He knew nothing about her background, or her personal life...

'Are you doing anything this evening?' he asked, and she looked up, surprised.

'No. Why?'

'I thought we could go out and celebrate.'

If he wasn't mistaken, she was blushing. Or it could have been wind-burn.

'Celebrate what?' she asked, laughing.

'All this – finally getting started. It's exciting.'

She nodded.

'It is, isn't it? Yes, OK, thank you. I'd like that.'

But not as much as he would, Toby thought as he made his way back to the house, Holly trotting at his heels for once.

Different worlds or not, Laurie Summerfield fascinated him.

Laurie absolutely refused to get herself in a tizz about an evening out with Toby Davis.

She had to concentrate on her work, find out all she could about the events surrounding her dad's conviction, and make sure no-one recognised her.

She certainly didn't have time to entertain thoughts about Toby.

So it mattered not a jot what she wore.

He'd seen her at her worst, clad in tatty waterproofs and wellingtons. Did she think she could bowl him over just because she was dry, clean and wearing a dress?

Why did she want to bowl him over? Because she'd been fascinated by him from the start?

She couldn't get over Toby growing into such an attractive man. She still struggled to believe he was so – nice, when as a child, he'd struck her as a bit spoilt. Stupid, too, if she were honest.

That was the last thing he was nowadays. Apart from having a fine business head on his shoulders, he was thoughtful, kind, considerate, willing to help...

Her phone rang.

'Hello, love, how's it going?'

'Dad!' She settled down for a good natter. She had plenty of time before Toby arrived.

'This is a nice surprise. It's going well, thanks. How are things with you?'

'Oh, can't complain.'

No, he never did...

Laurie told him how the work was coming along.

'Oh, and I thought Sally Mason had recognised me.'

She told him about the chat she'd had with Sally.

'And do you know what,' she added, 'I mentioned that to Toby, and he said Laura Whitney was all legs and teeth. Cheeky devil!'

Jim roared with laughter at that, and even Laurie had to smile.

'Actually–' She wasn't sure how her dad would react to this. 'He's asked me out to-night. We're going to celebrate the progress – well, the fact that we're about to start making progress.'

'Are you indeed?'

It was difficult to tell from Dad's tone

whether he approved or not.

'He's really nice, Dad.'

'Oh, I don't doubt it,' Jim said immediately. 'He always was a nice lad – his dad was one of the best, too. But don't forget, love, he has every right to feel bitter towards us.'

'But that's just it – he doesn't,' Laurie argued. 'Anyone with half a brain would know–'

'No,' Jim cut her off. 'All the evidence pointed to me. Never forget he lost his dad that night.'

It was difficult to put herself in Toby's shoes. How would life have been if her own dad had been killed when she was just thirteen – especially with no mother to help her through?

'Your dad was always there for you, Laurie, even if you couldn't see him as often as you liked,' Jim said quietly, and sharp tears sprang to her eyes.

'I know that, Dad.'

They talked of other things – Laurie's cottage, and the weather.

'I've just remembered,' Laurie said suddenly. 'Sally Mason was talking about a curate who went missing. Do you remember that?'

'I do – Alan Watson,' her dad said. 'Nice chap, he was. Just vanished.'

'So Sally said. Don't you think that sounds

a bit suspicious, Dad?'

'In what way?'

'Well, he could do a disappearing act, then come back and steal some jewellery. Who'd suspect a curate?'

'Laurie! For heaven's sake – what on earth would he want with jewellery?' Jim protested.

'Who knows? The same as you. He'd only been in the village a year or so, hadn't he?'

'Yes, but take it from me, Laurie, he was no thief.'

'So what happened to him?'

'I don't know, but I don't imagine it was good. I remember them searching the woods up there, and the hills.' He paused. 'There's something I do remember, though. One night – oh, it would have been about a month before the young chap vanished – Mr Edward had been working late, and he said to me, right out of the blue, "I'm worried about Alan Watson, Jim."'

'I asked him what he meant, but he dismissed it. Reckoned he was just being fanciful.'

'Dad!' Laurie was both horrified and fascinated. 'Didn't you think it odd when he vanished?'

'Of course I did. I asked Mr Edward again what he'd meant, but he was very tight-lipped. He murmured something about him – the curate, I mean – being depressed. If

74

you ask me, I reckon the poor chap might have done away with himself.'

Laurie wasn't convinced.

'You don't think there's a connection? His vanishing and then the trouble at the Hall?'

'No, and the police didn't, either.'

Laurie did. To her mind, the curate was chief suspect, and she was determined to find out all she could about Alan Watson. Still, there was no point telling her dad that...

When the call ended, Laurie returned to the mess that was her bedroom, and shook her head at the stupidity of it all. A grown woman, a divorced woman at that, ought to have more sense. Anyone would think she was a starry-eyed sixteen-year-old off on a first date!

Toby arrived five minutes early, in fact, and Laurie was pleased to see that he was dressed smartly, but casually. She was glad she'd settled on a simple dress.

He'd booked a table at a hotel about ten miles away. Laurie could remember driving past it.

The outside had appealed to her, but the inside was something else. It was quiet, warm, the tables were private, and the waiter was attentive.

'What a lovely place,' she said.

'Isn't it?' Toby agreed. 'It's just been bought

by one of the big chains. The food was always excellent, but now–' He shrugged. 'We'll see.'

The menu certainly made her mouth water, and she spent ages studying it. Finally, she settled on melon garnished with fruits, followed by pork sautéed with mushrooms, onion, cream and brandy. As ever, she was ravenous.

How bizarre it all was! If someone had asked her ten years ago, she would have thought herself more likely to walk on the moon than have dinner with Toby Davis.

They talked easily, about the Lancashire weather and the gardens at Kingsley Hall, until their food arrived.

Toby was a home-made soup man. For his main course, he'd ordered lamb marinated in rosemary and garlic.

Must remember not to kiss him, Laurie thought. The idea made her smile inwardly.

'Sally said you'd done a lot of travelling,' she remarked.

'Yes. I stayed on at school in England after my father died,' he explained, 'but I spent my holidays with my aunt and uncle. My uncle's in the diplomatic corps.'

'And after school?'

'Oxford. Then I spent a while in Saudi – still with my uncle.'

'And meanwhile, the Hall was becoming more and more overgrown?'

'Sadly, yes.'

He wasn't exactly forthcoming.

'Why didn't you come back before?' she asked, and he shrugged.

'There seemed nothing to come back to. I'd almost decided to sell the place, but when I came back to have a look, it felt like home.'

Of course – he hadn't seen the place since he was thirteen years old. It must hold very unhappy memories...

Laurie had been so wrapped up in her own problems, she kept forgetting Toby's – yet they were the same problems. Two lives had been changed for ever by the events of that night in 1985.

'What about you?' he asked briskly. 'Have you lived in Middlesex all your life?'

'Yes,' she lied.

He didn't like talking about himself, while she couldn't. What a disastrous evening this promised to be!

'What made you decide on horticultural college? Was it something you'd always wanted to do?'

She could hardly tell him she'd longed for university, but hadn't been able to afford that.

'When I saw details for the horticultural college, I thought I might enjoy it.' She smiled. 'Of course, I loved it. I made a lot of friends there, too.'

Including a husband.

'What about family?'

Ha! What indeed. *A father imprisoned for twelve years for killing your father. A mother who found the strain too much. An ex-husband without whose name I would still be Laura Whitney...*

'Just my father,' she said briskly. 'We're very close – he works in the hotel business.'

Toby could make of that what he wished.

The pork was superb, but Laurie's spirits had dipped. What was the point of spending time with someone when you couldn't be open and honest with them?

She had to clear Dad's name. Nothing else mattered. One day, Toby would find out that she'd deceived him, and she must accept that, not hanker for a friendship that couldn't be.

'Sally was talking about the curate who went missing,' she said, cutting into her meal. 'Do you remember that?'

'I remember hearing something.'

'It was a couple of months before the, er, burglary.'

'I've heard about it, but I would have been away at school at the time. I don't remember him.'

'What a strange business, to just disappear like that.'

He nodded, but didn't comment.

'What about when you're not designing gardens?' He changed the subject. 'What do you like to do?'

'Eat,' she said, and he laughed.

'Yes, I'd noticed your healthy appetite...'

They managed to talk of other things – books and music, films they'd both enjoyed – and Laurie found it amazing that they had such similar tastes. It made the evening much easier. And very pleasant...

A couple of weeks later, Laurie was peering down an old wellhead neither she nor Toby had known about. It was at the back of the house, near the orchard, and she and Toby, as children, must have ridden the ponies over it many times. How had they missed it?

It had been boarded over many years ago, and grass and weeds had hidden it. Now that the ground had been cleared away, it was clearly visible.

She wondered again how deep it was. There was no water in it; she and Dave had established that much.

'About twenty feet deep, I reckon,' Dave had said when they'd found it, and Laurie had to smile. How could he tell that, just by dropping a stone down and waiting for the thud?

Her mobile phone rang, and she saw from the display that it was her ex-husband.

'Do you fancy lunch on Saturday?'

Steve's question caught her off guard.

'Oh, well–'

'Come on, Laurie, no excuses! I've got a long weekend, so I thought I'd drop in on you on my way down.' He paused. 'Don't worry, I won't tell anyone I'm the ex-husband.'

'It's not that.'

But, of course, it was exactly that.

'That's part of it. I feel as if I'm on borrowed time.' She tried to explain. 'I told you about Sally almost recognising me? I don't want anyone suspecting I'm using my married name.'

'I know that, although I still don't like the thought of all the – deception.'

'Without the deception, I wouldn't have a job here. And you can think what you like, Steve, but you have to admit it's a dream of a job'

'I'm not arguing with that. It's just – oh well, we'll agree to differ.' His voice lightened. 'So then, lunch? It'll be my treat – as much sherry trifle as you can eat.'

She had to laugh.

'You know me too well. OK, Steve, thanks. I'll look forward to it.'

'Me, too.'

'Will you have time to visit Dad, do you think?'

Laurie knew her dad had missed Steve since he'd been working in Scotland, and he looked forward to his visits.

'Yes, plenty. I've already managed to see him on Sunday.' She caught the humour in his voice. 'Unlike you, he sounded as if he might be pleased to see me.'

'He will, and so will I. Stop fishing for compliments! Try and get here early on Saturday,' she told him, 'and I'll show you round the estate. Oh, my, I've always wanted to say that!'

'I'll be there as early as I can,' he promised, laughing.

They ended the call, and Laurie put her phone back in her pocket – or so she thought. She watched, horrified, as it fell into the well.

It hit the side twice and, if she wasn't mistaken, lodged itself on a stone. It was difficult to tell, as it was too dark down there to be sure. Was that her phone, or was it simply a stone sticking out?

Now what?

She could go out and buy a new one, but her whole life was stored on that one.

Could she get it? No, it was madness even to consider it. Twenty feet was a long way to fall – and for all she knew, it could be forty feet.

All the same, the stonework looked solid enough, and there were plenty of footholds. Given a rope, perhaps it wasn't as ludicrous as it sounded.

She strode off to the back of the stable block, and found Dave hard at work laying slabs.

'All right, love?' he asked, straightening up,

and again, she was struck by what a lovely man he was. She always thought of him as a gentle giant.

One of the nicest evenings she'd spent in Lancashire had been with Dave and his wife, June. She'd heard all about their four children, and shared their excitement at the imminent arrival of their first grandchild.

She also knew how grateful Dave was to have this job. He'd lost his previous one when a nearby farm had been sold, and had applied to be the estate's 'works manager' when Toby came home. He loved it.

'Not really,' she answered. 'Actually, I need a favour, Dave.'

'Name it.'

'Ah, well, it's not that simple. The thing is, I've dropped my mobile phone down the old well.'

'And you want me to go down there and–?'

'Good heavens, no!' She had to laugh as she pictured Dave's huge form on one end of a rope and her on the other. They'd both be in the well!

'No, I thought if I had a rope tied to me, and you on the other end of it, I'd be able to climb down. My phone didn't go far – it's lodged on a stone that's jutting out.'

She hoped!

'Aw, Laurie–'

'Will you come and have a look?'

'I'd rather give you a hundred quid to buy

a new phone.'

'Yes, but it's not–'

'That simple,' he finished for her. 'No, it never is. Come on then. Women! The bane of my existence…'

Half an hour later, with two strong ropes round her waist and under her arms, and a torch looped over her arm, Laurie was climbing into the well.

She couldn't fall, because Dave and Roger were hanging on to the rope, but her phone suddenly seemed less important by the second. There were plenty of footholds, but thanks to the recent rain, they were treacherous.

'Don't worry,' Dave called, 'we've got you. You can't go anywhere!'

His words reassured, and his torch gave out a good light…

There it was – her phone!

'Got it!' she called up, putting it safely in her pocket, and began the short climb back.

Her hand landed on something soft, frightening her. Investigating farther, she realised it was a cloth bag with something inside it.

Curious, she stuffed it in the other pocket.

'That was easy!' She let Dave hoist her on to solid ground again. 'I don't know what all the fuss was about.'

Dave looked at Roger.

'Women!'

'Ta-da!' She took her phone from her pocket to show them. 'Not a scratch on it. Oh, and I found this.'

She took the grubby cloth bag from her other pocket.

'Treasure,' she said, grinning.

The bag was starting to disintegrate, and even as she tried to open it, an earring fell to the ground.

No-one said a word. The three of them stared in disbelief as a diamond necklace landed on the grass at their feet...

CHAPTER FOUR

For the first time since Steve had arrived, and sitting at the table in the Ram, halfway between Todmorden and Burnley, well away from prying eyes at Kingsley Hall, Laurie fell silent.

As the waitress put their food in front of them, she realised just how hungry she was. Food had been low on her list of priorities this last week.

Even the sight of thinly-sliced roast beef and Yorkshire pudding couldn't distract her for long, though.

'It was a nightmare,' she told Steve, voice lowered. 'One minute I was looking at all those diamonds glistening at my feet, the next I was looking straight at Toby. He'd wandered over to see what we were doing.' She picked up her knife and fork. 'He didn't say a lot. I think he was even more shocked than I was, and that's saying something.'

Steve nodded, but he was still frowning.

A memory flashed into Laurie's mind. In the early days of their marriage, when they'd been madly, deeply in love, she'd imagined having Steve's children, and she'd wondered if they'd be born with that frown of his.

She'd wondered, too, if they'd be born with the same warm green eyes, and the freckles that were more visible on days like today when the sun was shining...

'I've heard nothing since,' she went on, pushing the memory from her mind. 'A policeman came to speak to Toby, and he had a quick chat with me when Toby was there, but it was all very informal. I haven't seen Toby all week.' She hesitated. 'Steve?'

'Mm?'

'I know the police are aware of all this, but do you think I should have a word with them?'

His eyebrows shot up at that.

'No!'

'But why not? Surely this puts a whole new light on things?'

'Of course it doesn't,' he said gently. 'It simply means – in the eyes of the police, at least – that whoever stole that jewellery panicked, and threw their catch into the old well. The fact that they'd been disturbed by Toby's dad, and had hit him so hard they'd killed him, must have sent them half crazy.

'There's a huge difference between a thief and killer. Imagine their mental state. They would have panicked, thought it was never worth it and thrown the jewels into the well. Perhaps they even thought someone had spotted them.'

Laurie couldn't argue with that.

'The jewellery's been recovered, that's all,' he went on. 'The police will make a note on their files and that will be that. I imagine the insurance company will be more interested than the police.'

Laurie knew he was right, but it rankled.

'What did your dad say?' Steve asked eventually. 'I assume you were straight on the phone to him?'

'He didn't say much at all. He was as shocked as I was. I think, though, that he was pleased, in a strange sort of way. As he said, at least people wouldn't imagine him living off the proceeds.'

'I wish–' Steve broke off.

'What do you wish, Laurie asked, curious.

'That you weren't involved in all this. I know it's painful, but it's ancient history, Laurie. All it can do is upset you, upset your dad – there's nothing you can do.'

At the moment, she didn't think there was anything she could do, but it wouldn't stop her trying.

'Your father wasn't the one to spend twelve years in prison,' she reminded him.

He looked at her, and the sympathy she saw there brought foolish tears to her eyes.

'I know, love,' he said, and his voice was softer now. 'I just worry about you getting involved.'

Laurie knew an almost overwhelming urge to fling herself into Steve's arms for a big hug. He was so dear, so familiar, such a good friend.

'So how's work?' he said, changing the subject.

Laurie told him of the progress being made at the Hall and, for a while, it cheered her to think of the gardens.

It was good to hear about Steve's work, too, but it didn't take her mind off those jewels – the jewels her father gave twelve years of his life for...

'Have I ever mentioned Martin Cooke?' Steven asked at last. Laurie thought he sounded a bit reluctant.

'The name rings a bell, but–'

'I was at school with him, but we lost touch for a while. A year or so ago, we met up at a wedding. Anyway, he's a lawyer – practising in Manchester.' He laid down his knife and fork. 'I could have a word with him, if you like.'

'Oh, Steve, would you?'

'Yes, but don't get too excited, Laurie. I'm sure there's nothing he can do.'

'I know that, but all the same…'

'And it would mean giving him the whole story,' he pointed out.

'I know that, too.'

She didn't want Toby discovering her identity, although she supposed one day, he would. She simply wanted – what did she want?

The truth. Some means of clearing her dad's name. And she wouldn't rest until she had that.

As she drove them back to her cottage, she felt more settled, and more optimistic, too. It had been good to talk things over with Steve.

'Sorry I haven't been very good company,' she said as he was leaving.

'You're always good company.'

If she wasn't mistaken, he sounded wistful. Was he, too, thinking of what might have been?

They both knew there was no point in that, though. They each appreciated their friendship, but they'd proved beyond any doubt that they weren't capable of anything deeper.

'Give my love to Dad.' She pushed her thoughts aside.

'I will. And I'll have a chat with Martin.' He held her close for a moment. 'I'll give you a call, Laurie. Take care.'

'You, too, Steve. And thanks...'

Toby Davis barely noticed the rain lashing his face, obliterating what should have been a stunning view of the Pennines.

He should be delighted that his mother's jewellery had been found after all these years. The police, assuming he was, had treated him as if he were a lottery winner.

The truth, though, was that Toby wished it was still at the bottom of that confounded well. Along with jewels, all the old painful memories had surfaced.

'Holly!'

The dog was barking at nothing, as far as Toby could see, but she immediately raced back to his side, her rare show of obedience taking him by surprise.

'Perhaps we'll make a normal dog of you yet,' he said fondly.

He hadn't thought about this until now, but he should offer Laurie a reward for finding the jewellery. He wanted to show his appreciation, but he didn't want to offend her. It was difficult.

Perhaps he might think more clearly if he could push the memories aside for more than five minutes at a stretch, and if he could get rid of all this anger.

As it was, every time he thought of that confounded butler... Somehow, it was worse to know that his father had been killed for nothing.

His father had trusted Jim Whitney, treated him like family. Even that daughter of his had been given the run of the Hall. She'd gone on family outings, attended Toby's birthday parties, been allowed to ride his ponies...

Toby was a great believer in accepting whatever life threw your way, and moving on, but at times, it was difficult.

It was also difficult not to feel bitter. How different his own life would have been if they'd never known Jim Whitney.

Not that life had been all bad. His aunt and uncle had been kindness itself, and had always done what they'd thought right for him. He'd wanted for nothing – that money could buy.

How he wished his father was here now! They could plan the future of Kingsley Hall together...

Thinking back, he'd been surprised by Laurie's reaction on finding the jewellery. She'd been shocked, obviously, but that hadn't entirely explained her unusual silence.

From the moment she'd arrived, she'd been fascinated by everything about Kingsley Hall, especially tales of the burglary. Yet she hadn't said a word about finding his mother's diamonds.

Sally Mason, on the other hand, hadn't stopped talking about it. His housekeeper was full of talk of the Whitney family and the events of that November night twenty years ago.

He'd been avoiding her this last week, and he'd been avoiding Laurie, too, for much the same reason.

He must have walked for miles since Laurie had handed him that disintegrating cloth bag with those cold stones inside it.

He'd tramped half the Pennines, and hadn't even noticed their beauty...

'Come on, Holly,' he said. 'Time we headed home.'

By the time they got back to the Hall, the rain had stopped and the sun was trying to shine. Deciding he could avoid Laurie no longer, and knowing only a fool would want to, he set off to find her.

'She's down by the lake with the contractor,' Dave told him.

Toby thanked him, and set off in the opposite direction.

As he walked, he visualised the sunken rose garden that was to be, and the main walk with its herbaceous borders. It cheered him a little.

Laurie was indeed by the lake, and the sight of her made him smile for the first time that day.

She was an expressive talker. As she spoke to the chap who was going to dig out part of the lake, her arms were pointing to this and that. The contractor, cap in his hand, was scratching his head in bewilderment.

Toby sympathised; when Laurie was in full swing, there was no keeping up with her.

'Toby!' She gestured for him to join them.

'We were discussing the lake,' she explained, 'and Bob here – oh, sorry. Bob, this is Toby Davis, the owner of the Hall. Toby, Bob's firm is going to sort out the lake for us.'

Toby shook hands with Bob. They'd met before, but Laurie clearly didn't know that, and neither of them was likely to get a word in to enlighten her.

'I know we'd planned just to alter the shape of the island, Toby,' Laurie rushed on, 'but I feel that, while we're at it, we ought to sort out the mess there.'

She pointed to the far side of the lake.

'With that straightened out – well, a curve put in, to match this side – it would give a more pleasing shape, don't you think?'

Toby could see immediately what she meant.

'I do,' he agreed. 'It's fairly straightforward, isn't it?'

'I suppose so,' Bob replied thoughtfully. 'Someone will need to give us the proper measurements, though. Once we've dug it out, it'd be difficult to change.'

'No worries,' Laurie assured him. 'Dave and I will measure it up and get it marked out. For the island,' she added, looking at Toby, 'I think we should aim for the same curved shape.'

She took some crumpled sketches from her pocket.

'I was working on these last night.'

The three of them spent almost an hour discussing the new ideas, and Toby's spirits were higher than they'd been for days – since his mother's jewellery had been found, to be precise.

'He's a nice chap,' Laurie commented as Bob went back to his car.

'He is,' Toby agreed.

Now they were alone, she seemed edgy, or was it his imagination? Perhaps he was edgy enough for both of them.

'Actually, I wanted a word with you, Laurie,' he began as they walked back towards the Hall together.

'Oh?'

Edgy and defensive.

'Yes. I haven't had a chance to speak to you since last Monday, and I wanted to thank you for – well, if it hadn't been for you, my mother's jewellery would have been lost for ever. I'm very grateful.'

'You must be glad to have it back after all these years,' she said, in a tight little voice, 'and I'm glad we found it. Not that it had anything to do with me,' she rushed on. 'All I was worried about was my mobile phone. If Dave hadn't been willing to help me get it back–'

'Well, I'm grateful,' he said, 'and I'd like to – what I mean is, there's a reward – obviously. The jewels–'

His voice trailed away, silenced by her expression.

'A reward?' Her face was deathly pale, dominated by huge, startled eyes.

'Of course. At today's value–'

'Oh, no!' She carried on walking, so quickly that Toby was struggling to keep up with her.

'But you must,' he insisted, confused. 'From a purely financial angle–'

'Toby!' She sounded furious. 'I have no interest whatsoever in the financial angle. I'm glad the jewellery has been found, but that's it. I'm here to design the gardens. I certainly don't want – couldn't–' For once, she was lost for words.

'Excuse me, but I need to see Dave.'

With that, she ran off ahead. She actually ran away!

'What the devil was all that about?' Toby murmured in amazement.

Laurie didn't know what to expect from Terri Marshall. Like most folk, she supposed, she'd never met a real private investigator before and, when they'd spoken on the phone, she'd been taken aback to realise it was Terri, and not Terry.

'Expect me to be wearing a raincoat with upturned collar, dark glasses, false moustache – oh, and I'll have a camera slung over my shoulder.'

Perhaps Terri's attempt at humour was her way of trying to put Laurie at her ease. She must have sounded nervous...

True to his word, Steve had spoken to his friend, the lawyer. Martin Cooke had phoned Laurie, which was good of him, and she'd warmed to him immediately.

'Sadly, Laurie, there's nothing I can do. There isn't any new evidence, you see.'

Really, she'd known he would say that.

'What I suggest is that you speak to a private investigator. I know of one who's very good – ex-CID – and I can give you a contact number if you're interested...'

So here she was, sitting in the lounge of the Holiday Inn, waiting for a female wearing a raincoat with an upturned collar...

She had a good view of the reception area, and she watched people coming and going. None looked like private investigators.

Then one young woman spoke to the receptionist, and strode towards Laurie. In casual trousers and blouse, she was no older than Laurie, wore her long hair tied back and had an easy smile on her face. Instead of a camera, she had a brown leather handbag slung over her shoulder.

'Laurie Summerfield?' Her handshake was full of confidence.

'Terri Marshall?'

She nodded, then grinned.

'What do you think of the disguise?'

Laurie had to laugh.

'Coffee?' Terri asked.

While they waited for their coffees, they chatted about the weather, the local motorway network, and about Terri's work.

'With the police so overworked,' she said, 'more and more people are employing private investigators these days.'

As soon as coffee was in front of them, Terry took a notebook from her handbag and asked Laurie to tell her all she knew.

Laurie did, starting with everything her dad had told her, recalling her own memories, and bringing Terri right up to date with the finding of the jewellery.

Terri made very few notes and didn't interrupt once.

'I was hoping the police might get involved,' Laurie confided. 'You know, set one of these cold case units on it.'

Terri smiled at that.

'You've been watching too much television,' she said. 'A very small number of police forces have what they call review departments that delve into old cases.

Instructions come from the Home Office, and it's usually a case that might he helped by more advanced forensic techniques.'

'Oh.'

'In this case, as far as the police are concerned, it's cut and dried. The crime has been solved. Even better, the stolen goods have been recovered.'

'Yes, but – well, there are two things. Firstly, my father is innocent.'

She wasn't sure she liked the expression on Terri's face as she said that, but she chose to ignore it.

'Second, as far as I can tell, no-one thought it odd that, only a couple of months earlier, the local curate chose to do a disappearing act.'

'The curate?'

Laurie told Terri about Alan Watson, and how Toby's father had told her dad that he was 'worried' about him.

'Don't you find that suspicious?' she asked, but Terri shrugged. 'It would be easy,' Laurie went on, 'for him to do a disappearing act, then frame my father for the burglary. Who'd suspect a man of the church?'

'I know where you're coming from,' Terri murmured, but she didn't look convinced. 'Another coffee?'

Laurie nodded.

This time, Terri drank her coffee thoughtfully.

'Laurie,' she said at last, 'you know your father is innocent, and your father knows it. Isn't that all that matters, in the end? If you start delving into the past, all you'll do is drag up unpleasant memories and, more likely than not, suffer your father being branded a thief and a killer all over again. Is that what you want?'

'No.' Laurie was determined. 'What I want is my father's name cleared. It ruined his life, and it ruined my mother's life.'

She gazed at Terri steadily.

'It didn't do much for my life, either.'

'I can understand that, but–'

'As far as I'm concerned, it will be worth whatever price has to be paid.' An involuntary shudder ran through Laurie as she spoke. What price was she willing to pay? 'It's obvious to me that the police overlooked something.'

'It's a long time ago, Laurie.'

'I know that.'

Terri put her cup down and gazed at Laurie for several moments.

'OK,' she said at last. 'I don't think there's anything I can do, but I have to admit I'm intrigued. I'm owed a couple of favours by the local police force – and my husband's still in CID – so I'll see what, if anything, I can get my hands on. I make no promises, Laurie, but I'll see what I can find out.'

'Thank you.' Laurie meant it.

'I'll have to talk to your dad, of course,' Terri said.

'I'd rather you didn't,' Laurie said at once. 'Not yet, at any rate. Until it's absolutely necessary, I'd like him kept out of it. He's suffered enough.'

'I can imagine. OK,' Terri said, 'we'll leave that – for now.'

She frowned suddenly.

'Was there a reward for finding that jewellery?'

'Oh, don't!' Laurie grimaced at the memory. 'Toby spoke to me about it and I was so – oh, I thought for a minute that I was going to be sick. Neither of us has mentioned it since.'

'Pity,' Terri murmured, eyes brimming with humour. 'My services don't come cheap, you know…'

Laurie laughed, as was expected, but her mind was still on Toby and the atmosphere between them.

Toby must be thinking he'd employed a madwoman. Who in their right mind would turn down a reward?

Now, they couldn't even talk about the gardens without that awkward atmosphere between them, and Laurie missed their chats.

'Can I come to the Hall and have a look round?' Terri asked. 'You can invent some story – say I'm an old schoolfriend, or something.'

'Of course. And thanks, Terri.'

Laurie was relieved. She had the feeling that Terri believed her story, believed her dad was innocent, and was as keen to solve the puzzle as Laurie was.

At last, Laurie felt as if she had an ally.

A week later, Terri Marshall was sitting in her new house, surrounded by notes she'd made on the Whitney case. She should have been unpacking yet more boxes, but this case intrigued her for some reason.

Perhaps it was because she'd liked Laurie from the start. She liked her honesty, and her determination to clear her dad's name.

If it were Terri's own dad – well, she couldn't imagine how she would feel. Devastated, at best.

Sadly, Jim Whitney wasn't the first man to be wrongly accused. He wouldn't be the last, either.

The missing curate intrigued Terri, too, as did the fact that, of the people she'd spoken to about him, several had mentioned Alan Watson's dealing with a local lawyer, Daniel Armstrong. Mr Armstrong, it seemed, had also vanished into thin air.

Daniel Armstrong was beginning to intrigue her even more than the curate. According to people she'd talked to, he had been either loved or loathed. Some hadn't a bad word to say about him; others referred to him as hypocritical and two-faced – with a penchant for fine wine.

The thought of wine sent Terri to the kitchen, where she found a solitary bottle of cheap white plonk. Unlike Daniel Armstrong, she and Adam, her policeman husband, couldn't afford fine wine.

Lawyers were often condemned, though, she knew that. When faced with their accounts, people often believed solicitors had a licence to print money.

Having said that, Terri had discovered one local woman, Kathleen Eve, had been so impressed with Daniel Armstrong that she'd remembered him in her will, much to the chagrin of her daughter.

'Conned, she was. "Only friend she had," she reckoned. Huh! Wasn't him who cooked, cleaned and–' She'd broken off on a sob, and shown Terri photographs of herself with her children and her mother in happier times.

'He used to be a hot-shot in a big practice in Manchester,' Linda explained, 'but he moved out to Kingsley. He helped Mum with her will, and persuaded her to borrow money on her home – as if she needed to. Of course, he took a nice cut...'

The question was, where was Daniel Armstrong now?

He'd left Kingsley in April, 1986, less than six months after the burglary. No-one, it seemed, had a clue where he was now, if indeed he was still alive.

And what about the curate?

'A nice chap, Alan was,' Kathleen Eve's daughter had said. 'Always kind and helpful. It's a mystery what happened to him. Not that I knew much about it – it was only a few months after Mum died, you see...'

A curate vanishing into thin air and a lawyer disappearing off the face of the earth! It was all very odd.

'And probably irrelevant,' Terri muttered to herself.

She wished she could talk to Jim Whitney, but Laurie was right; her dad had been through enough.

One day, Terri would have to speak to him, but it could wait.

Meanwhile, she sorted through the photographs of Kingsley Hall she'd managed to take when Laurie had showed her round...

More than two hundred miles away, Jim Whitney's thoughts were also focused on Kingsley Hall.

He was lying in bed, knowing sleep would evade him. He suspected he'd witness the sunrise yet again as thoughts of that long-ago November night haunted him.

There was something he was missing, something they'd all missed.

Why hadn't he seen or heard an intruder that night? It would have been impossible for someone to get in without him knowing about it. He would have sworn to that.

Who the devil had got in, opened the safe, killed Mr Edward?

And another thing, why had Mr Edward been hit from behind? Surely, if he'd come downstairs and disturbed the burglar, he'd have been hit at the front of the head, not the back. Even the police hadn't been able to come up with a satisfactory explanation for that one.

Jim got out of bed, pulled on his clothes, and went downstairs to make himself a cup of tea. So much for his early night, and anyway, he fancied a drink.

He hadn't been feeling too good lately. There was nothing he could put his finger on, but he wasn't feeling one hundred per cent … and he was constantly drinking tea.

It was probably this constant remembering, he decided. It wasn't good for a man.

All those nights in that cell – he'd spent every one of them going over these events and trying to put the pieces together. Then, when freedom, or a sort of freedom, had been his again, he'd done his utmost to put it all behind him.

Now, with his daughter at the Hall, and the surprise discovery of those jewels, it was impossible. He could think of nothing else.

For his own part, it no longer mattered. If a miracle happened and they found the real culprit, it couldn't help him now. It couldn't give him back those twelve years, nor could it bring back his lovely Anne.

It was young Laurie who mattered now. She was everything a man could wish for in a daughter, and he loved her with every breath in his body. What had she ever done to deserve a father for ever labelled a thief and a killer?

It made his blood boil every time he thought of it, and he thought of it every single day...

He glanced at his watch. Not even nine yet! Perhaps his mate Micky fancied putting the world to rights...

Jim drank his tea, then got to his feet. He would walk round to Micky Reagan's. If his friend wasn't in, or wasn't in the mood for visitors, it wouldn't matter. At least the fresh air and exercise would do Jim good.

As he walked, it struck him again that he didn't feel particularly well. The evening was warm and dry and couldn't have been better for a walk, yet every step was an effort. What on earth was wrong with him?

Lack of sleep, probably.

Lights shone brightly from Micky's house, and Jim's ring was answered almost immediately.

'Hi, mate, come on in,' Micky said, his face alight with pleasure. 'You would not believe the rubbish I've been watching. What brings you here anyway?'

'Oh, just thought I'd take a walk,' Jim told him as he followed him inside. 'It's a lovely night.'

'Fancy a beer?' Micky asked.

Strangely, Jim didn't, yet he still had a raging thirst.

'I'd rather have a cup of tea.'

'Tea it is, then.'

As Micky made the tea, Jim sank down at the kitchen table. There was a thin film of sweat on his brow, and he really was thirsty.

'You OK, Jim?' Micky asked curiously. 'You look a bit washed out.'

He'd always been straight with Micky, and he always would be.

'To tell the truth, I don't feel great,' he admitted. 'Just lately, I can't seem to settle at all. I'll go to bed exhausted, sleep for an hour, two at the most, and then be wide awake again.'

Micky nodded in sympathy.

'Come on,' he said when the tea was made, 'let's go and sit in comfort. I'll switch this confounded thing off,' he added, prodding the TV's remote control.

'So, what's keeping you awake – or need I ask?'

'Oh, the usual questions,' Jim told him. 'Questions that I doubt we'll ever have the answers to. I suppose it's been worse since the jewellery was found at the Hall. All these years, I've been wondering who'd taken it, whether they'd broken it up and sold it, who'd bought it, what the thief had done with the money, whether that thief had ever thought about me, and had a good laugh at my expense. Now, though, it's thrown me. Those jewels never left the Hall! What made the thief throw them in the well? Did someone spot him? Was it the same person who phoned the police to say the Hall was on fire?' He shook his head in despair.

'So many questions, Micky, and not a single answer.'

'I must admit I've been giving it a lot of thought myself.'

And between them, they didn't have a single answer.

'There's something wrong with the whole thing,' Jim persisted.

'We're overlooking something, I'm sure of it.'

'Like what?'

Jim had to smile.

'If I knew that, I wouldn't be overlooking it.'

The smile was short-lived.

'Oh, my–'

It came to him in a blinding flash.

All these years, everyone had thought about the burglary. That's what they'd all been made to think about.

The burglary had simply been set up to throw them off the scent. It hadn't been a burglary at all! It had been murder.

His heart was racing as fast as his mind now.

Mr Edward had been murdered, and it had been made to look like a burglary that had gone wrong.

He was about to tell Micky all this when a sudden, crushing pain in his chest robbed him of breath. He clutched at his chest – it felt as if a ton weight had landed on him.

As if from a great distance, he heard Micky say he was calling an ambulance.

Jim could neither agree nor argue. The pain was crushing the life from him...

CHAPTER FIVE

'What are you doing here?' Jim Whitney looked up in amazement from his hospital bed. 'I made a point of telling Micky–'

'Charming!' His daughter dropped a kiss on his forehead. 'I drive over two hundred miles to bring my dad a bunch of grapes, and this is the thanks I get.'

It was a huge relief to see him looking as well as Micky had promised.

'And where are these grapes?' he asked

knowingly, and she laughed.

'I haven't actually bought them yet. So how are you, Dad? Truthfully!'

'Truthfully, I feel as fit as flea.' He reached out for her hand. 'I had a funny turn at Micky's house and didn't feel at all well, but that's passed. There's certainly no need for all this fuss.'

'That funny turn was a heart attack, Dad,' Laurie pointed out.

A fairly minor one, hopefully, but there was no point telling him of the conversation she'd had with the doctor. Dr Adams had said that they still had tests to do, but it did seem as if it was a warning, and that no real damage had been done.

If she told her dad that, he'd see it as a licence to carry on as normal.

'So they say,' Dad muttered.

'And what does Doctor Whitney believe it was?'

'Probably nothing more than indigestion,' he growled. 'Certainly nothing that warrants all this fuss. Unless I discharge myself, I have to–'

'Discharge yourself? Don't you dare!'

'I won't, I won't. But I don't relish the thought of being stuck here for days, either – and they are talking days, Laurie.'

'Of course they are.'

They needed to do more tests, to establish what had caused it, and to see if surgery was needed – though Dr Adams said it was un-likely.

Whatever the results showed, her dad would need plenty of rest – and no stress in his life.

Laurie was torn. She didn't know whether she should persevere in her quest for the truth, when she'd probably get nowhere. Or whether she should offer Toby her resigna-tion, and put it all behind her.

The best medicine Dad could have was his name finally cleared, but what would the stress of it all do to him in the meantime?

'What about you, love?' he asked. 'I hope Micky didn't tell you to come dashing down here in the middle of the night.'

'You know him better than that. He phoned to let me know what had happened, so I thought I'd drive down and see you. I was in the midst of arranging a few days' holiday anyway,' she lied.

'Hmm.' Clearly, he wasn't convinced.

'Get a good night's sleep,' Micky had sug-gested on the phone, 'and drive down in the morning.'

A good night's sleep when her dad had been rushed to hospital?

Laurie had stopped long enough to throw some things in a bag, and dash up to the Hall to tell Toby where she was going.

'The truth, now, love,' Jim persisted. 'What does young Toby really think about you abandoning your work on a whim? Not very professional, is it?'

A whim?

'He was wonderful. He even offered to drive me down here.'

Jim's eyebrows shot up.

'I declined his offer, obviously, but I did appreciate his kindness.'

In fact, Toby's kindness and gentle concern had caused her to drive for at least half an hour with tears in her eyes.

Amazingly, his first reaction on hearing the news had been to pull her close and give her a much-needed hug. That hug had done something to her, something she was too emotional to think about just now.

She couldn't ignore the fact she wished he were with her, though. Toby Davis had grown from a slightly spoiled, pompous boy into one of those men you could lean on. At the moment, Laurie would have loved to lean on him.

Still, no use thinking along those lines. She could just imagine his reaction on arriving at the hospital and being taken to Jim Whitney's bedside.

Dad's eyes were closed now, and she guessed he was worn out.

Laurie couldn't help blaming herself for this. She should never have gone to the Hall in the first place! As everyone was so fond of telling her, the past was better left alone.

All she was doing was making life worse for everyone. If she hadn't gone back to Kingsley Hall, Toby's mother's jewellery would still be at the bottom of the well, her dad would be sitting happily at home, she wouldn't be living a lie, and she wouldn't be having ridiculous thoughts about Toby Davis...

'Laurie,' Jim said eventually, opening eyes that were surprisingly bright and keen. 'Before this happened, when I was at Micky's, I had a thought.'

He seemed reluctant to go on.

'And?' Laurie prompted.

'About what happened at the Hall that night. I don't think it was a straightforward burglary at all,' he told her. 'No, the more I think about it, the more I think–'

'Yes?'

'I think it was murder, Laurie. I think someone wanted Mr Edward dead, so they made it look like a burglary that had gone wrong...'

'What do you think?' Terri Marshall asked her husband.

'I think we should get out in the fresh air,' Adam replied briskly. 'It's a lovely evening. Come on, get those walking boots on.'

He was right; it was a waste to be indoors. Besides, she loved walking, and often did her best thinking while she was in the countryside.

They set off, arm in arm, up the hill. It was good to be away from houses and traffic.

'So what do you think about Laurie's theory?' Terri persisted after a while. 'That it might have been murder, not burglary at all?'

'I think I should have married someone with a proper job and, more importantly, a proper salary. I hope you're getting well paid for this, love, because I can see it claiming your time for months, years even.'

Terri knew he was only teasing. In reality, her husband was very supportive and always had been.

'I also think,' Adam went on, 'that you don't know for sure Jim Whitney is innocent.

'I know you like Laurie, but for all you know, he's simply convinced her he's innocent. He could have been responsible for the whole thing – the bungled burglary, the murder–'

'I don't think so.'

'I know you don't,' he said, smiling indulgently, 'but how do you explain the bundle of cash delivered to him?'

'I can't,' Terri admitted, 'and neither can he. He was framed, no doubt about that.'

She thought back to her phone conversation with Laurie. Laurie reckoned that her dad was ill because of stress. He thought of nothing else these days.

'If worrying about all this has put him in

hospital with a heart attack,' Terri pointed out, 'it stands to reason he's innocent.'

'Or he's worried his precious daughter will stumble across something to prove his guilt! Look, love, he was a butler. I doubt if the pay's anything to write home about. And he loved his wife and daughter – right? Well, wouldn't he want more for them? Wouldn't it be tempting – seeing that jewellery every day, knowing it was only gathering dust in a safe? He knew the house, and he knew his boss's habits – probably better than anyone else.'

'If that were the case, how do you explain that bundle of cash?'

'OK, so he was put up to it.' Adam thought for a moment. 'He couldn't do it himself, perhaps, but if someone offered him good money to steal it – well, it's easy money, isn't it?'

Terri shook her head.

'No, I don't buy that. There are too many missing links. There's the puzzle of the missing curate – and Laurie's dad said that Edward Davis had been worried about the man.'

'He might have invented that to focus attention on the curate. I can't see that being anything to do with it.'

'So there's the mystery of the cash, the way the victim was hit from behind – and while I agree that the curate probably has nothing to do with it, there's also the lawyer. Where has he vanished to? There's no trace of him at all.

'One thing's certain,' she added grimly, 'if Daniel Armstrong is still alive, he must be worth a few bob. I've heard of several folk who remembered him, often very generously, in their wills.'

'A perk of the job, I suppose.' Adam shrugged.

Usually, Terri liked throwing ideas back and forth with Adam. She was familiar with his work, and he'd been at her side ever since she'd left the force to set up as a private investigator.

On this case, though, he wasn't being much help, because unlike her, he wasn't convinced of Jim Whitney's innocence.

Adam was more logical, more practical, while Terri was inclined to trust her instincts.

He hadn't met Laurie, either. When he did, and Terri hoped Laurie was to become a good friend, she felt sure he'd feel just as strongly as she did.

Of course, Adam could be right – Jim Whitney might have managed to convince his daughter of his innocence.

Terri would dearly love to meet him, and she felt sure it would be helpful, but Laurie was adamant, and Terri respected her wishes. With Jim in hospital, Laurie would be even more determined to keep them apart.

The Marshalls walked, hand in hand, to the reservoir. Rabbits raced around, enjoying the sunshine, and several geese flew in to land on the water. The birds clucked and squawked, fighting over what looked like a tiny piece of bread on the lake, before settling down. As they splashed, the water glistened like diamonds in the late evening sunlight.

'It's lovely here,' she remarked, 'but I do envy Laurie, living in Kingsley. It's a heavenly little place, right next to the Pennines.'

Adam gave her a sharp look.

'We're never, ever, moving house again. Remember?'

Laughing, she punched him playfully.

'It wasn't that bad.'

'It was a nightmare.'

The house move had been stressful, she had to admit, and of course, it wasn't practical to live too far out of Manchester. All the same, she'd love to live just ten or twenty miles farther north.

She'd like a dog, too. The more she thought about it, the more she liked the idea. Now that they had a garden, and decent-sized house, it was feasible. The dog would be company for her, too. She'd be able to take it on her travels with her.

One of their neighbours had a collie that was about to have puppies. Maybe she'd take Adam along to have a look at them. Surely even Adam wouldn't be able to resist a young puppy...

They walked down the hill towards home.

'Fancy a drink?' Adam asked outside the pub.

'Why not? I haven't heard the local gossip lately.'

Their local, the Green Man, was a hotbed of gossip, but unfortunately, or perhaps fortunately, most of it was pure fantasy.

It was busy, as usual for a Saturday night, and as soon as she had a drink in her hand, Terri was grabbed by Carol, their neighbour.

Carol was fascinated by Terri's job. No matter how many times she tried, Terri couldn't convince her that it wasn't the glamorous lifestyle Carol imagined.

Having promised they'd get together some time, she rejoined Adam at the bar.

He was skimming through a newspaper, and she reached his side just as he was about to turn the page.

'Oh, no!' She grabbed the page to stop him turning it over. 'Look!'

It was a small paragraph on page five. The headline was *FREED KILLER IN HOS-PITAL.*

'*James Whitney, fifty-nine,*' Terri read out in a whisper, *sentenced to twelve years for the manslaughter of Edward Davis in 1985, was admitted to the North Middlesex Hospital on*

116

Thursday evening–'

'I wonder if Laurie's seen it,' Adam murmured, frowning as he read on.

'I don't know.'

'And what about Toby Davis?' Adam put in. 'Would he read this, think about Laurie racing down to Middlesex to see her sick father, and put two and two together?'

'More than likely. He's not stupid.' Terri had a sick feeling in the pit of her stomach. 'I need to speak to this reporter, and find out what I can from him. I just hope he doesn't try to contact Jim about all this! That's the last thing the poor man needs...'

That evening, Laurie and her dad walked to the hospital cafeteria for a coffee.

'I shall be glad to see the back of this place,' Jim muttered.

'Oh, you! A life of luxury you've had – waited on hand and foot, nurses chasing round pandering to your every whim.'

He laughed at that.

'Aye, they've been very good.'

'They have, so stop complaining.'

Laurie was relieved to see her dad looking so well, and delighted to know he was fit enough to go home the following day. All the same, she knew that this warning couldn't be ignored.

'You will remember to keep these appointments, won't you, Dad? It's important you're checked out regularly for a while.'

'I will.'

Laurie was fairly confident he'd do as he was told, and she knew Micky would keep a close eye on him.

'And no work until the doctors give you the go-ahead,' she reminded him.

'I won't. I'm sure the hotel will cope without me.'

'They'll have to!' she said firmly.

She'd spoken to the manager personally. He was a lovely man, and he'd promised Laurie that her dad would be sent packing if he showed his face there.

'And don't forget to take your tablets,' she added.

'Ha! That'll be a full-time job. I've got about eight a day – I'll rattle.'

After their coffee, Laurie walked back to the ward with him.

'Try and get a good night's sleep, Dad, and I'll see you in the morning.'

He'd been on the treadmill that morning, and she knew the fact that he hadn't heard the results was worrying him. He didn't want anyone to tell him anything other than that he was very fit and healthy...

Laurie had a couple of phone calls to make, and she stepped outside to switch on her mobile phone.

She'd missed three calls, one of them from her ex-husband. Steve's phone was engaged.

She guessed he was calling to see how her dad was, as she'd only spoken to him last night.

Terri had also left a message, asking Laurie to call her, but her mobile was switched off. No answer from the Marshalls' home phone, so Laurie left a message.

Then she spoke to Micky, who was just about to nip over to her dad's flat and make sure it was all ready for him.

'Don't you worry about him,' Micky said. 'I'll make sure he does as he's told...'

Laurie hit the button for Toby's number. She'd spoken to him early on Saturday morning, and had promised to update him.

'Laurie! How are you? How is your father feeling?'

The display on his phone must have told him who was calling, and his obvious pleasure warmed her. It reminded her of the way he'd hugged her before she'd left for Middlesex.

'I'm fine, thanks, and Dad's doing well. He's going home tomorrow, all being well, so I should be back with you on Wednesday morning.'

'That's excellent news. What a relief! I bet he's pleased.'

'He is. Busy moaning about all the tablets he has to take, but glad to be going home.'

Toby laughed at that, and Laurie knew a sudden sadness. He and her dad would get along well, she was sure of it, yet they would never meet.

'Actually,' she went on, 'I was going to ask a favour, Toby.'

'Ask away. If there's anything I can do.'

'I've ordered a couple of books off the internet, and they might have been delivered today. Unless Tommy knows I'm away, he'll leave them outside–'

'Tommy?'

'The postman.'

'Is that his name?'

'Yes.' Laurie had to smile. 'Anyway, he'll leave them by the front door, but if it rains, they'll be ruined. Would you have a look for me and put any parcels somewhere dry, please?'

'Yes, of course. Is there anything else I can do?'

'Nothing, thanks. I'll see you on Wednesday, then, all being well.'

'Yes. See you Wednesday.'

The sudden silence between them was not uncomfortable, far from it. Was Toby as reluctant to end the contact as she was?

'Er, right, 'bye then, Laurie.'

''Bye, Toby.'

As soon as he ended the call, Toby strolled down to Laurie's cottage, marvelling at the beauty of the day. It was chilly now, but it had been a warm day. Everywhere still looked fresh and clean after last night's rain.

Better still, Laurie was coming home on Wednesday. Until she'd gone, he hadn't realised just how important she'd become to him...

He cut through the back garden and, sure enough, there was a parcel waiting. A couple of books? Unless they were huge tomes, there were half a dozen. Laurie was an avid reader, he knew that much.

He unlocked her front door and put the parcel on the table just inside. There was a heap of mail, mostly gardening magazines, and he put that in a neat pile beside it.

It struck him then just how much he loved the look she'd given the cottage. There were faded flowers in vases on almost every surface. He spotted at least three opened books balanced here and there.

The shrill ring of the phone suddenly broke the silence, startling him.

'Hi, you've reached Laurie Summerfield's number. Sorry, I can't take your call right now, but leave a message and I'll get back to you as soon as I can...'

Even the sound of her voice on the machine was a pleasure. He was longing to talk to her again.

Her caller was speaking now.

'Laurie, we keep missing each other. I've tried your mobile, but it's switched off again – you must be inside the hospital. Anyway, just to update you – I've finally traced the vicar and I'm going to see him and find out what he knows about the missing curate. Give me a ring, will you, so we can discuss this? And a bit of bad news, I'm afraid. I don't know if you've seen today's paper, but your dad's made the nationals. I hope he doesn't read "The Globe". I hope, too, that reporter doesn't try to contact him while he's in hospital. He's served his time – he doesn't need this raked up again. OK, I'll try your mobile again, but if you phone in here to check your messages beforehand, give me a call...'

Toby, his mind racing, locked up the cottage and strode back to the Hall, untouched now by the beauty of his surroundings.

What had that been about – the missing curate? Laurie's father having – what did that female say? 'Served his time'?

Sally took 'The Globe'. He'd seen this morning's edition in the kitchen.

When he reached the Hall, Sally was nowhere in sight. It didn't matter; the newspaper was still lying on the dresser.

Toby opened it and flicked quickly through the pages. He found what he was looking for at the first attempt.

The words leapt out at him.

James Whitney ... sentenced to 12 years ... admitted to the North Middlesex Hospital on Thursday evening ... always protested his innocence...

'Here, young Toby!' Sally strode into her kitchen. 'Don't go throwing that paper out. I haven't had time to read it yet.'

'Then you might like to read this, Sally,' he said grimly, prodding at the offending article.

With that, he strode out of the kitchen, too angry to talk.

Wednesday was one of those days that made you glad to be alive, Laurie decided. The sun was shining from a clear, blue sky, and everyone was smiling. Drivers seemed more polite and less hurried than usual.

She'd seen Dad settled back at home, left him in the capable hands of Micky, and started the drive back to Lancashire first thing this morning.

And there it was – her cottage. She was home.

As soon as she unlocked the door, she saw Toby had put her parcel inside. He'd picked up her mail, too.

She was tired after the drive, but she was also eager to get to the Hall and see what progress had been made in her absence. The work on the lake had been delayed, she knew that, but it might have started today.

She'd have a quick shower, then go up to the Hall and see for herself.

Laurie's answering machine was blinking and she hit the 'Play' button. She'd spoken to Terri since that message had been left, yet it still made her heart skip an uncomfortable beat.

Thankfully, the reporter hadn't contacted her dad while he was in hospital, but Jim had read the article.

'They can print what they like about me,' he'd said, shrugging it off, 'but what about you, Laurie? What if Toby's read this?'

That hadn't even crossed Laurie's mind.

'So what if he has?' she'd said. 'All he knows is that I'm visiting my father in a hospital in Middlesex. He doesn't even know which hospital, and even if he did, no doubt several people's fathers will have been admitted last Thursday evening...'

There was nothing to link her to Jim Whitney, but now she was home, the thought of the deception brought a bitter taste to her mouth.

Occasionally, when she was feeling optimistic, she could console herself that, when she'd proved her dad's innocence, she could tell Toby the truth and all would be forgiven.

Half an hour later, after a quick shower, she was more or less ready to go. She made herself a coffee while she looked through her mail.

A cream envelope caught her eye. On the front, in familiar, bold, dark writing, was her name: *Ms L. Summerfield.*

She ripped it open, and stared for a full minute at the single sheet of Kingsley Hall headed notepaper.

I would be grateful if you could report to my office at 4 p.m. on Wednesday. If this is inconvenient, please telephone me to arrange a time.

T. Davis.

CHAPTER SIX

Any hope this meeting might have been to do with anything other than her identity faded as soon as Laurie saw the anger in Toby's eyes. He was polite – too well brought up to be anything else – but she could almost touch his anger.

Laurie couldn't blame him. She'd lied to him, knowing full well what his reaction would be if he discovered who she really was.

Even his study, a room that had always touched her with its warm homeliness, now seemed cold and forbidding.

'I can explain,' she began, but she wasn't given the chance to complete the sentence.

'I can tolerate most things.' He cut her off, tapping a pen on his desk. 'I can't tolerate dishonesty. You, Ms Whitney – it is Ms

Whitney, isn't it?'

'It's Ms Summerfield,' she said quietly. She wished he would stop tapping that pen; her nerves were ragged enough without that.

'I suppose no-one can blame you for changing your name.'

'Most women do when they marry,' she retorted.

The pen stopped tapping, but her nerves didn't stop jangling. He was looking at her now, and she couldn't read the expression on his face.

She shouldn't have been so abrupt, but his comment had infuriated her. She was proud of the Whitney name – proud of her father.

Silence stretched between them.

'That's neither here nor there,' he said at last. 'You've been less than honest with me.'

'I have, but–'

'And I'm dispensing with your services,' he continued, talking over her attempt at an excuse. 'I'd like you out of the cottage by the end of the week. I'll pay you for your services for the next three months. I think that's fair.'

He picked up an envelope and thrust it at her.

'I've already written the cheque.'

Laurie wasn't sure what brought the sting of tears to her eyes – whether it was losing her job, the fact that he was being generous financially, or knowing she'd lost Toby's trust, respect and friendship.

'I wasn't completely honest with you,' she admitted.

Dark eyebrows vanished beneath equally dark hair at that.

'You weren't!'

'But I had my reasons.'

'I'm sure you did. I have no interest in them.' He got to his feet. 'There's nothing left to say.'

Again, he attempted to hand her the envelope.

'I'm not a charity case,' she said hotly, on her feet now. 'You can keep your cheque, just as you can keep the reward for those jewels. I never wanted money.'

'There's nothing more to say. There is your cheque. Take it or leave it. If you'll excuse me–'

'You might have nothing to say, but I have plenty, and I'd be grateful if you'd do me the courtesy of listening.'

He let out a sigh and sat down again.

'I'm listening,' he snapped.

'Yes, I'm Laura Whitney – or was. I'm the "scrawny thing – all legs and teeth", as you put it. However, I am now Laurie Summerfield, and I'm well respected in my field. My ex-tutor approached me about the work here – I didn't even know it was at Kingsley – because of a design I'd submitted for an exam. He thought my ideas would suit your house. Not surprising really, as I'd had the Hall in mind when I came up with the original designs. When he told me the job was here, working for you, my first thought was to forget all about it.'

'Then it's a pity you didn't.' Again, he rose to his feet.

'However, I came here for two reason,' she continued. 'Firstly, I have always loved Kingsley Hall. Some of the happiest days of my life were spent here. Secondly, I had ideas of discovering the truth about what really happened the night your father was killed.'

'The police, the court, the jury – they all know what happened that night.' His voice was as cold and empty as his eyes.

'And they're all wrong.'

He stared back at her. The look on his face said it wasn't worth arguing.

'That night, you lost your father and your life changed completely. I lost mine, too. Oh, not in the same way you did. My father was alive – he was simply locked up in a cell, away from the wife and daughter he loved. My mother struggled to live like that – if it hadn't been for me, I don't know what she would have done. She died within a year of him coming out of prison. You once asked why I chose horticultural college. I didn't. I longed to go to university, but there wasn't the money for that.'

She took a breath. 'I know you're not interested in my problems, and I don't blame you, but I'm simply trying to say that my father lost everything that night. He couldn't take care of his wife, and he couldn't watch his daughter grow up. What was much worse, was the knowledge that you believed him to be a thief. A thief and a murderer.'

'I'm sure he doesn't lose sleep over that.'

The scathing tone of his voice was too much for Laurie.

'You fool,' she cried. 'He would have died for your father!'

He leaned back in his chair.

'Don't you know that?' she shouted. 'He adored Mr Edward. Even now, he has nothing but good to say about him. He was so grateful to him – for putting him through college, taking him on as butler, treating his family like – well, like family. He worshipped your father. No way would he have killed him.'

'It was an accident, I know. My father was unfortunate enough to disturb him when he was–'

'Rubbish!'

Toby rose to his feet once more. He was certainly impressive, Laurie thought grimly. Impressive, forbidding and unapproachable.

'What happened twenty years ago,' he said

calmly, 'has nothing whatsoever to do with the current situation. I won't tolerate dishonesty from my staff – or from anyone else. As I said, I'd like you out of the cottage by the weekend.' He glanced at his watch, but Laurie doubted he knew what time it was.

'Now, if you'll excuse me, I have an appointment...'

He strode past, leaving her alone in his study.

'Aren't you frightened I'll steal a pen?' she yelled after him.

There was no response, which was probably just as well.

Early the following morning, Laurie and Terri Marshall were walking by the old reservoir in Bacup.

In the shadow of the Pennines, the reservoir was now a nature reserve where, despite a sign asking people not to feed the ducks, bread was being scattered on the water. Ducks and geese squabbled noisily over each tiny crumb.

'Let's walk along the path,' Terri suggested. 'I'm intrigued to see where it goes.'

They set off, with Laurie kicking a couple of stones in front of her.

'So what are you going to do, Laurie?'

'What can I do, other than pack? I have to be out of the cottage by the weekend.'

'I can see his point,' Terri said quietly.

'I suppose I can, too,' Laurie admitted. 'What I can't see is his refusal to consider the possibility that my father just might be innocent.

'For heaven's sake, I can remember his father, just about, and I'm younger than Toby, so he must remember Dad! He must know how things were – that Dad wouldn't have harmed a hair on his father's head.'

'But when all the evidence suggests otherwise–'

'I suppose so.'

In Toby's position, Laurie hoped she would be more open-minded.

'All Toby will have heard was that his father was killed by the butler,' Terri went on. 'He won't have considered anything else, because there has never been a need to. You've considered it because of your dad – how is he, by the way?'

'He's doing well, thanks.' Laurie brightened momentarily.

'He just refuses to listen – Toby, that is, not Dad. He's so – blinkered!' She huddled deeper inside her jacket. It wasn't cold but she felt chilled.

'Anyway, there's no point in my going on and on about it. Sorry.'

'Don't apologise. I can see you hardly had any sleep last night.'

She was right. The unfairness of it all, and Toby's refusal to listen to reason, had preyed on her mind all night. On top of that, of course, was the sadness at having to leave Kingsley.

'You said you had news,' Laurie reminded her.

'Yes. You knew I was going to see the vicar yesterday? The one who was here when Alan Watson was curate?'

Laurie nodded.

'Well, for a vicar, he struck me as a distinctly unhelpful character. I didn't take to him at all.'

They walked under the bridge, shivering as water dripped on to them.

'He knew nothing about the curate,' Terri continued, 'other than that he simply took off without telling anyone, and he certainly wasn't interested in discussing the night when Toby's father was killed. As far as he was concerned, it was cut and dried. Your father was responsible and got what he deserved.'

She gave Laurie a weak smile.

'He doesn't sound hot on forgiveness, our vicar.'

'So he was no help at all,' Laurie said flatly.

'Not really, no,' Terri admitted. 'Although he did talk about the lawyer, Daniel Armstrong. He reckoned he and the curate were as thick as thieves. I still can't trace him, though.

'However, there's more news. You remember that fine arts chap, Charles Taylor? The one your dad remembered calling at the Hall a couple of weeks before the burglary, saying he had an appointment with Toby's father?'

'The man who didn't exist? Yes.'

'Charles Taylor might not exist, and the address he gave was certainly fake–'

'The police established that,' Laurie reminded her.

'Yes, but a Charles Taylor – giving that same address – booked into a hotel in Burnley around then.'

'No!' Laurie's mind was racing. 'So he does exist! Well, someone claiming to be the fine arts expert, Charles Taylor, exists.'

'Yes. That's the good news,' Terri said carefully. 'The bad news is that we have no description – nothing to go on. And it's twenty years ago.'

That, of course, was their main problem. It had happened so long ago that people had forgotten all about it, and no longer cared.

'Laurie, I really need to talk to your dad. Perhaps he remembers something else about Charles Taylor – something that would help. He might remember what he looks like – anything.'

Laurie groaned.

'What a mess,' she said. 'I haven't even told Dad that I've been kicked out yet! I'll drive home tomorrow – probably late, because I need to pack everything up and – well, there won't be room for it all in my car. Or I might give my old flatmate a ring and see if she can help.'

Laurie knew she had to accept the facts. All she'd done so far was pack a few clothes. It was as if by doing nothing, she could ignore the fact that she had to leave Kingsley Hall, but she needed to let people know what was happening.

'When I see Dad at the weekend, I'll tell him you'd like a word. At the moment, he doesn't even know I've spoken to you. He wants his name cleared as much as I do, but he isn't keen on my getting involved.'

'OK,' Terri said. 'And don't worry, Laurie. If your dad does agree to speak to me, I won't say anything to upset him.'

'I know that. Thanks.'

'Hey cheer up! Something will turn up.' Terri squeezed her arm.

They walked on in silence for a few yards.

'So what will you do, Laurie? I know you're going back to Middlesex, but what then?'

'Fortunately, I didn't give up the lease on my flat, so I'll go back and get on with my life. I'll find another job – soon, too.'

It wouldn't be at Kingsley Hall, though.

'And you do want me to stick with this, don't you?'

'Yes. Yes, I do.' Laurie was firm about that.

'Thanks to Toby, I'm more determined than ever to get to the bottom of this. I want Dad's name cleared, and I'll stop at nothing to achieve that.'

'For your dad's sake?' Terrie asked knowingly.

'Of course.'

There was more to it than that now, though. Yes, Laurie wanted the world to know her dad was innocent. She wanted him to be able to hold his head high once more. And she wanted to prove Toby wrong.

She'd thought – hoped, at any rate – that he might be able to keep an open mind. Apparently not.

'You really liked Toby, didn't you?'

'I did, but I suppose I always knew he'd want me out of his life if he found out who I was.'

At the moment, she didn't want even to think about Toby. His dismissal had hurt more than she cared to admit. The way he'd called her 'Ms Whitney' – oh, that had hurt. Just as his coldness had hurt.

'I still have lots of packing to do,' she went on, forcing a smile. 'In the short time I've been here, I seem to have accumulated a lot of stuff. Thankfully, I still have lots of boxes, but it'll take me ages to pack up all my books.'

'What about the gardens at the Hall?' Terri asked. 'Will Toby bring someone else in?'

'I imagine so. Yes, of course he will. Now that we've sorted out the basics, anyone could take my place.'

That hurt, too. Someone else would see the public come through the gates for the first time and admire her rose garden, her herbaceous borders, her lake. Except they weren't hers. They were Toby's.

'Will you come back to have a look – as a member of the paying public, I mean?'

'No!'

Laurie never wanted to return to Kingsley Hall.

'Now, young Toby,' Sally began sternly, 'we need to have words about this dog of yours. I can't have it in my kitchen. You'll have to keep him out.'

'I will.' Toby, looking up from his cup of coffee, knew there was no point in telling Sally yet again that Holly was female. Right now, the dog was the last thing on his mind, but he'd have to try to keep her out of Sally's kitchen.

'So long as you keep the door shut, Sally–'

'The wretched creature opens the door!' Sally put her hands on her hips and glared at him. She was positively looming, Toby thought, as she frowned down at him, sitting on the sofa.

So he got to his feet.

'Then I'll do my best to keep her out of

the way,' Toby promised.

How he'd do that, he had no idea. At the moment, he didn't much care, either.

'So then—' Sally said.

Toby looked at her, waiting for more.

'What's going on?' she asked. 'I saw young Laurie this morning and she said she'd been dismissed!'

Toby supposed he should have seen that coming.

'That's right.'

And what sort of man would be answerable to his housekeeper, in any case?

'You can't do that.' Sally sounded appalled.

'Did *young Laurie—*' he emphasised that '—tell you why she'd been dismissed?'

'She did, but I can't see that's reason enough to get rid of the girl.'

'What? She's been totally dishonest—'

'Not really,' Sally said. 'Her name's Laurie Summerfield. She's well qualified to do the job she's doing. There's no law that says a girl has to tell her employer what her dad was once accused of, or that she shouldn't use her married name.'

Toby was amazed. He'd thought that Sally, who'd been employed at the Hall for more years than he cared to remember, would have some loyalty to the family.

'Her father killed my father,' he said flatly.

'No.' Sally shook her head. 'Jim Whitney didn't kill your father.'

'Oh, so you've had a good long chat with Ms Summerfield!'

'I've had nothing of the sort,' Sally retorted. 'The poor lass was too upset to say much. She only told me the reason you'd sacked her.'

'What makes you so sure Whitney wasn't responsible for the burglary and my father's death? Do tell, Sally. After all, you must know something that the police don't know, that the jury wasn't told–'

'I knew Jim Whitney,' Sally said, ignoring his sarcasm. 'I knew his wife, Anne, and I knew young Laura. They were a good family, and he was loyal. He'd worked for your father for eighteen years before – before that night.'

'Perhaps it would have been better all round if he'd simply asked for a salary increase! No doubt my father would have been good enough to oblige. God knows, he bent over backwards for that family. That – Laurie Whitney–' he was struggling to say her name '–even rode my ponies.'

'She did,' Sally agreed. 'A better rider than you she was, too. I remember all that – the way she used to wait down by the gate when you were coming home for the holidays.

'All morning she'd be there, up with the lark, no matter how many times we told her you wouldn't be here until after lunch.' Sally shook her head, a half smile playing on her lips. 'She'd wait and she'd wait – and then you'd ignore her.'

He certainly didn't remember that. All he could remember was that his father had thought the world of her – of the entire Whitney family. Jim Whitney's father had been gardener at the Hall, for heaven's sake!

'My decisions are my own, Sally.' Toby knew even as he spoke that he sounded pompous. 'I won't tolerate dishonesty, and that's that.'

'It's a good job you're not in her shoes.' Sally nodded in the vague direction of the cottage.

'And another thing—'

Toby couldn't believe he was standing here listening to his housekeeper telling him right from wrong.

'Supposing he was guilty? He wasn't, of course, but for the sake of argument, suppose he was? Is that any reason to get rid of young Laurie? Surely not. It's a long time since we've had to be held accountable for the sins of our fathers! When you gave her the job, I very much doubt if you put a clause in the contract about instant dismissal if you didn't approve of her father. In fact, I very much doubt if you gave her a contract. I've been here for forty years, and I've never seen such a thing.'

She chuckled.

'Just as well, really.'

It was just as well. The way he felt today, he would have had Sally out on her ear!

'Master Toby,' she said, and her voice was warmer now, gentler, too. 'I can imagine how you feel – how all the memories hurt – but can't you give Laurie a chance?'

'No, Sally, I can't. For all I know, she could be planning to steal–'

'Steal what?' Sally retorted. 'The jewellery she found in that horrid well, and handed over to you?'

'Well–' Toby had no answer.

'I was only thinking last week how good Laurie Summerfield was for you,' she went on. 'She has a soft spot for you, no mistaking that. I thought you might feel the same.'

'Nonsense! You do realise, Sally, that she's Mrs Summerfield? She's married. Neither of us is in any position to have a soft spot, as you put it.'

'Divorced,' Sally said patiently.

'Divorced?'

Any second now, Toby was going to lose his last shred of patience – not with Sally, but with himself.

All his life, well, for as long as he could remember, he had been a sensible, practical sort of person whose head ruled his heart. So why had his heart suddenly leapt at hearing Laurie was divorced?

If he were completely honest, the worst part of that interview in his study had been the moment she'd said she was married. That had robbed him of speech.

'Married too young, apparently,' Sally said, 'but she's still good friends with her husband. Nice chap, he sounds. He's working in Scotland on a conservation project.'

'I'm very pleased for her,' Toby said, the sarcasm – and a twinge of jealousy – taking him completely by surprise.

'I think, Master Toby, you'd do well to think how different things will be around here when she's gone.'

And Sally left him to himself.

For the rest of the day, Toby did exactly that.

He took Holly for a long walk over the hills – at least it would keep her out of Sally's kitchen – hoping that the exercise would calm him down.

It didn't. The exertion quickened his heartbeat, already going at a frightening pace.

'Holly, for–!' He let out his breath on a sigh. 'Sorry, didn't mean to snap. It's not your fault, is it? Nothing worse than people taking their problems out on dumb animals.'

He stroked the dog's ears.

'Come on, then. Let's find a stick and I'll do an hour's stick-throwing penance...'

The problem was that he could throw a stick and dwell on this awful situation at the same time.

It didn't matter whether Jim Whitney was

guilty or innocent. He didn't for a second believe the man was innocent, but that was by the by.

What did matter was that Laurie had lied to him, made a fool of him, just as her father had made a fool of his.

He knew she wasn't planning to steal anything, of course. The idea was absurd. She was completely trustworthy...

Trustworthy? He'd dismissed her because of her dishonesty!

What was all that about her having a soft spot for him? Was Sally right about that?

Their friendship had developed into something more meaningful, there was no denying that. Yet all the time Laurie had been lying to him.

He'd thought it uncanny from the start that she should be as enthusiastic about the plans for the Hall as he was. How could she love the place as much as he did?

Well, now he knew. She said it was because she'd spent the happiest days of her life there.

Perhaps she had.

Toby's childhood had been privileged, but thanks to the generosity of his father, so had hers. A pity Laurie's father had been greedy enough to want more. Toby's anger surfaced all over again.

He believed all his dreams had been shattered, but they hadn't. He still had the Hall, and the gardens would still be something he would enjoy showing to the public.

Nothing had changed. So why did it suddenly seem so meaningless?

Why could he cheerfully raze the place to the ground?

Early on Saturday morning, Laurie was in a complete mess. Sheena would never know how grateful Laurie was.

Her flatmate had driven up from Middlesex and stayed the night, ready to help move Laurie's stuff today. She was currently enjoying a lie-in.

Laurie hadn't been able to sleep and now was alternating between fits of frustration, and a terrible emptiness that had her in tears.

Sally had called in to bring a box of supplies – home-baked fruits pies and cakes, and a casserole to put in the oven when they reached their flat.

'It'll save you doing anything.' Sally's smile seemed wistful.

The woman's kindness had almost reduced Laurie to tears again.

Laurie, not knowing what else to do, put on the kettle and made them tea. Now, they were sitting drinking it, unable to find words.

'This is a sad day.' Sally broke the silence. 'No doubt about that.'

'It is.'

Sadder than Sally would ever know. Laurie had already seen the digger go along the drive. This morning, the lake was finally being dug out, and she wouldn't be there to see it...

'I've had a word with young Toby,' Sally said, lips thinning, 'but he's as stubborn as a field full of donkeys.'

Laurie smiled at the description.

'I don't suppose you can blame him, Sally. I wasn't honest with him – he must hate the Whitney name.'

'Huh!'

Laurie didn't know what to make of that. Fortunately, she was saved from responding by the appearance of Sheena, in her dressing-gown, but wide awake.

Laurie introduced the two, and they chatted about the provisions Sally had kindly brought, and then the journey back to Middlesex.

While the other two were chatting, Laurie was watching the driveway to the Hall. Dave had stopped Toby's 4 x 4 in the drive to talk briefly. Their discussion over, Toby drove towards the cottage at a breakneck pace.

He screeched to a halt outside, jumped out, not bothering to shut the door after him, and raced up the path.

The next thing they knew, he was hammering on her door. When Laurie opened it he didn't wait to be invited inside.

'Whatever's the matter?' Sally asked him in amazement.

He was breathing heavily. He ran his hands through his hair in an obvious attempt to calm himself.

'You'd better come with me, Laurie,' he said.

She had a dozen questions, but the state he was in prevented her from voicing a single one. Instead, she climbed into the 4 x 4.

He didn't start the engine immediately.

'They started digging out the lake this morning.' His face was deathly pale.

'I know. I saw the digger.'

'They've found–' He turned in his seat to look at her. 'They've found a body.'

'What?' Laurie stared at him.

'Dave's phoned the police. They're on their way.'

'But – I mean – a body?'

Toby started the engine.

'I know nothing else,' he said, driving towards the Hall. 'Dave is very shaken, and it takes a lot to shake him. He said he thought it had been there a long time, but–'

He sighed. Toby, too, was very shaken, Laurie thought, and she herself was battling against urges to burst into tears, or scream loudly and never stop.

As he switched off the engine, they both

heard a police siren.

'I thought–' Toby cleared his throat and tried again. 'When Dave told me what they'd found... Dear Lord, I thought it was you!'

CHAPTER SEVEN

The beauty of the June morning was wasted on Laurie. She sat at the bench in her garden, an untouched coffee on the wooden table in front of her, and gazed up at the hills. She'd deliberately turned her seat around so she wouldn't be facing Kingsley Hall.

She'd been thinking of rhododendron, some of the large hybrids that would suit Kingsley, but what was the point? Someone else would deal with that now.

When she heard a car pull up, she went to the front of the cottage, expecting to see her ex-husband, Steve, climbing out. Instead, Terri greeted her.

'No news,' Terri explained quickly, 'but I had to be in Burnley early this morning, so I thought I'd call here on my way back and see if there was a coffee going spare.'

'There is.' Laurie was glad of her company. 'I'm sitting in the garden with mine...'

She made fresh coffee and they took it out into the garden.

'You're still here then,' Terri said.

'If I wait for Toby to tell me whether I should stay or go, I'll wait for ever. I've more or less decided I'll go up to the Hall and tell him I'm leaving now. What's the point of hanging around here like a spare part?'

To say the shock of learning that a body had been found in the lake had worn off wouldn't have been true. Laurie still shuddered every time she thought of it, but it was Toby's problem.

She should have driven back to Middlesex with Sheena, but the gruesome discovery had meant the day just vanished.

That evening, Toby made a request.

'Toby asked me to stay until things were sorted out, as he put it,' Laurie said, 'but I can't hang around here for ever with nothing to do. I've done no work, obviously. How can I when, officially, my employment has been terminated? And now it's Tuesday.'

The frustration, and yes, anger, were getting to her.

'Have you heard anything about it, Terri?' Laurie knew her husband was a policeman.

'Not really. I know it was a man's body, and that it had been in the water for years, rather than weeks or months. Going through missing person reports will take ages.'

Laurie nodded.

'They've sealed off a lot of the grounds while they search for – well, I've no idea what they're searching for. They don't look as if they have, either!'

She gave Terri a rueful smile.

'You'll have to excuse my bad mood. I'm not used to being idle.' She sighed.

'I'm so wrapped up in my own problems, I keep forgetting that some poor woman – a wife, a sister or a daughter – is going to face some very bad news.' She shivered, and pulled her shirt tighter around her.

'But I'll have words with Toby later. I'm neither use nor ornament stuck here.'

'I wish I had some good news for you, but I don't,' Terri said. 'I'm drawing a complete blank with our Charles Taylor.'

Laurie wasn't surprised. It was good to know that her father hadn't imagined the man. The Charles Taylor who checked into the hotel in Burnley had to be the same man who'd claimed he was an antiques expert, with an appointment to see Mr Edward.

'He must be connected with the burglary at the hall,' she said aloud.

'Oh, I don't doubt it,' Terri agreed. 'I just wish I could find out more about him. But there's still hope. People tend to use aliases that mean something to them – a relative's name, their mother's maiden name, something like that. Chances are if he used that name once, he'll have used it again.'

Laurie had agreed that, once she'd gone south, Terri would come and visit her and chat to her dad about all this. She sighed.

It was twenty years since he'd seen the bogus fine art dealer. Even if he could give Terri an accurate description, the man would have changed a lot in twenty years. He might even be dead by now!

'I'll keep checking,' Terri promised, 'and I'll let you know the minute I have any news.'

Just then a vehicle slowed to a stop outside.

'That will be Steve,' Laurie said.

'Your ex?'

'He's making a flying visit to his parents, and said he'd call in for a quick coffee on his way. And it will only be a quick coffee,' she added, 'so don't go dashing off.'

It was bliss to be on the receiving end of Steve's hug. He was so familiar, so dear, so – normal. Laurie craved normality at the moment. Since coming to Kingsley Hall, it seemed as if her life had been anything but.

'Come and meet Terri. What about food? Are you hungry?'

'No, thanks. I stopped at the motorway services for a big breakfast.'

Laurie introduced them and then went inside to make coffee. When she took it out, they were chatting as if they'd known each other all their lives. Terri was naturally curious about people, and Steve would get along with anyone...

'So what's it like being unemployed?'

Steve asked Laurie, and she pulled a face.

'Don't! Apart from the fact I don't have anything to do, I've been living out of a suitcase since Saturday. Sheena took a lot of my things back to the flat, but my other stuff is all packed and ready to go.'

'Why exactly does Toby want you here? That's what I can't understand.'

'When they found that body on Saturday, it was hectic to say the least. Everyone was shaken, and the police were asking all sorts of questions – about the house and the grounds mainly.

'I think he wanted me to help answer all the questions, sort Dave and the rest of the gang out, and show the police where we'd been digging and why.'

'That makes sense,' Terri said.

'Yes, but it's all done now. Presumably, when the police have finished checking the grounds out, Toby can get my replacement in.' She emptied her cup. 'Oh, and Dad doesn't know I've been sacked,' she warned Steve. 'I want to tell him face to face when I get home. I haven't told him about the body, either, because he'll start thinking trouble follows me around.'

She was beginning to believe that her-self...

Later that morning, Laurie walked up to the Hall. She hadn't seen Toby go out, but there was no sign of his Land-Rover.

'He's only nipped into town,' Sally told her. 'He won't be long. Come into the kitchen and keep me company.'

Laurie followed her through.

'Have some strawberries,' Sally nodded at a bowl on the table. 'They used to be your favourites.'

'They still are,' Laurie said with a chuckle, amazed that Sally remembered.

'You'll be staying with us then?' Sally remarked.

'Oh, no. Toby asked me to stay until – well, until the police have gone, I suppose. But no, I shall soon be heading home.'

Except her flat no longer felt like home. This was home.

'When I asked young Toby how long you'd be here, he spoke as if you were staying.' Sally shook her head in frustration. 'He doesn't seem to know what's happening! I reckon he's regretting sacking you.'

'I don't think so, Sally. Like everyone else, the discovery at the lake has taken his mind off everything else.'

She was sure Toby wanted her out of his sight as quickly as possible.

'Oh, I know. I still can't believe it. The number of times I've walked past–' Sally shuddered, 'To think of someone drowning in that lake – maybe when I've been here, in my kitchen. Dear me, you never know what's round the corner, do you?'

'You don't, Sally.'

'And how's Jim keeping?'

Since Sally had taken her side against Toby, Laurie's dad had become little short of a saint in her eyes.

'He's doing well,' Laurie told her. 'Still complaining about all the tablets he has to take, but at least he's taking them.'

Sally laughed.

'He was always as fit as a flea when he was here,' she recalled. 'Strong, fit, no weight on him.'

'There's no weight on him now,' Laurie said fondly.

'You were the same,' Sally went on. 'You used to race around here all day along. Nothing tired you out. You didn't stop from morning till night.'

'Happy days.'

'They were.' Sally sounded wistful. 'Of course, I always knew that Jim had nothing to do with Mr Edward's death. I just knew it. Toby should know it, too,' she added grimly.

'Everyone thought Dad was guilty,' Laurie said. 'There's no reason Toby should believe otherwise.'

'There's every reason,' Sally argued. 'Even folk who believed it at the time, meeting you, would know the truth. You're just Jim Whitney's daughter through and through.

That man's no killer! Folk only have to look at you.'

Laurie was so touched that she felt a stab of tears. But just then the front door opened, so she took a deep breath and pulled herself together.

'I'd better go and find him.'

She was about to do just that when mayhem broke out. Toby came into the kitchen with his dog and Holly, despite Sally's frantic shouting, had soon helped herself to half a bowl of strawberries.

'Get that dog out!' Sally shouted.

'Yes, yes.' Toby hauled Holly off the table and clung tightly to her collar as she pretended to look apologetic. 'Could I have a word, Laurie?'

'Yes, of course.' She followed him into the hall, where Holly promptly lay at his feet, a picture of devoted obedience.

'I think we need to talk,' Toby said. 'Would you have lunch with me, please?'

'Well, yes.'

'I've told Sally I'll be out. Will the Farrars Arms be all right? Or would you prefer somewhere else?'

'That's fine.'

She was hungry, and she wanted to find out when she could leave, but where she ate was unimportant.

They were both quiet as he drove to the Farrars Arms.

Laurie remembered when she visited the pub with Sheena on her first day here. She'd been worried then about Toby's reaction when he discovered her true identity. At least she had the answer to that particular worry.

They were both well known in the village now, and several people greeted them before they managed to get to a table.

The locals, as was to be expected, were all talking about the body in the lake. It was a long time since Kingsley had been the subject of media attention.

'Perhaps we should have gone somewhere else,' Toby remarked with a wry smile as they finally sat at their table.

'You can't blame people for being curious. It's shaken the whole village.'

'I know, and I wasn't.'

She was being abrupt with him, but she couldn't help it. In any case, he'd been less than polite when he'd dismissed her.

'Contrary to what you might think, Toby,' she began, 'I'm perfectly happy to accept your decision, but now it's been made, I'd like to be allowed to carry on with my own life as soon as possible. I'd like to go home today.'

'Today?' He seemed surprised. 'And what do you mean – "contrary to what I might think"?'

'You thought I was so distressed by your

decision that I'd thrown myself in the lake,' she pointed out, voice laden with sarcasm.

'I didn't think at all. I just thought – well, perhaps an accident. You were obviously upset, and–'

'Yes, I was upset, I always am when people call my father a killer.' Her chest was hammering with anger at the memory.

'Let's not argue,' Toby said quietly.

'I don't want to argue,' she assured him, as calmly as she could. 'I'd just like you to know that I want to leave this afternoon. Sad and shocking though the discovery of that body was, it's really nothing to do with me. I need to get on with my life again. I need to find another job.'

The girl came to take their order, and Laurie gave her a smile that was all at odds with her temper. She hadn't even looked at the menu, but she chose quickly.

When the girl left them alone, Laurie waited for some response. Toby fiddled with his napkin for a few moments.

'I'd like you to stay for a while,' he said at last.

'Why? The discovery of the body has changed nothing.'

'It's changed everything,' Toby argued. 'When Dave told me what they'd found in the lake – yes, my first thought was that it was you. I simply panicked. You see, I care about you, Laurie, and, for one reason and another, both of us have known more than enough tragedy in our lives. Like it or not, what happened twenty years ago has had a huge effect on our lives.' He paused.

'Perhaps this has made me realise we were just children at the time, and none of it was our fault. All I know is that I don't want any more tragedy.'

Laurie didn't, either, but she still couldn't see what that had to do with her staying on.

Their food arrived, which gave her an excuse to mull over his words.

They ate in silence, both lost in their own thoughts, but Laurie did notice that her pork was delicious. It was cooked to per-fection, and with lashings of delicious apple sauce.

Toby was first to finish, and when Laurie put down her knife and fork, her plate clean, she felt obliged to thank him.

'That was very nice, thank you.'

'I'm delighted to hear it. I suppose it's too much to hope that it's improved your mood?'

She almost smiled.

'Can I tempt you to dessert?' he asked. 'You never know, it might even make you civil.'

She did smile at that.

'The profiteroles might do the trick,' she said casually. 'I noticed a lady eating some as we came in…'

When Laurie had eaten her profiteroles, and Toby had polished off the largest helping of blackberry and apple crumble that she had ever seen, they sat quietly with coffee in front of them.

'I'm sorry if I seem angry,' she said at last. 'But I am. Your father was killed, Toby, and I sympathise with that. He was a good man; everyone says so. I remember him, too, you know. He always had time for me, and I remember him finding the best apples for me. So you lost a good, kind father and for that, I'm sorry. Now, if my father had died, and if dozens of people had attended his funeral and agreed what a good man he was, I could have coped. What I can't cope with is his being branded a thief and a murderer. My father is the kindest, gentlest, most loyal–'

She broke off, on the verge of bursting into tears.

'I'm sorry.' Toby's gentle tone did nothing for her emotional state.

'Will you stay?' he asked after a while.

She looked at him.

'We both want to see the gardens restored to their former glory,' Toby pointed out. 'We were working so well together, Laurie. Of course,' he added grimly, 'nothing can be done until the police leave the place alone, but I would like you to continue working at the Hall.'

Her thoughts were in turmoil.

'Will you at least consider it?' he asked, and she nodded.

'I'll think about it.'

'Thank you.'

That, she thought as they walked out of the Farrars Arms, was half the problem. Even the way he said 'thank you' had a strange effect on her.

She had two choices. Either she left Kingsley Hall and returned to her old life in the hope that she would get another job fairly quickly, or she stayed on, doing a job she loved, knowing her employer considered her father guilty of theft and murder.

One day, her father's name would be cleared, she was sure of it. In the meantime, however, she wasn't sure that she could work for someone who had such a low opinion of him.

They arrived back at the Hall just as a car pulled up. 'The police again!' Toby grimaced. 'I wonder what they want now?'

They'd spoken to Detective Superintendent Phillips on Saturday, and now he introduced them to his colleague, Detective Sergeant McGrath.

'We've identified the body,' he said. 'A Mr Alan Watson, who was–'

'Alan Watson?' Laurie broke in. 'The curate?'

Three pairs of eyes were fixed on her but no-one spoke.

'Do you know Mr Watson?' Detective Superintendent Phillips asked at last, frowning.

'Well–' She looked at Toby, huge eyes dominating a pale face. 'He was the curate who vanished before–' Her voice trailed away.

'Perhaps we ought to go inside,' Toby suggested. He had a feeling this was going to be a very long story.

They went into the sitting-room.

'You were about to tell us about Mr Watson?' the detective reminded Laurie.

'I only know he went missing about twenty years ago,' Laurie said. 'I lived here before–' She looked at Toby, and he saw the desperation in her eyes. 'My father, James Whitney, was butler at the Hall.'

Oh, yes, it was going to be a very long story.

'How did you identify him?' Toby asked.

'Surprisingly easily,' the sergeant said. 'He wore a gold cross around his neck. It had been inscribed, a confirmation gift from his parents. This was in the original report.'

'I see. So he committed suicide? Here at the Hall?'

'No, sir,' Phillips said grimly. He turned again to Laurie. 'Would you mind telling us all you know about Mr Alan Watson?'

'I don't know anything really,' Laurie admitted. 'I was only eight at the time. However, as I said, my father was butler here at the Hall in those days. You perhaps remember the case.'

She cleared her throat, and Toby saw the way her shoulders went back.

'There was a break-in at the Hall, and Mr Edward – Toby's father – was killed. My father spent twelve years in prison.'

'That's news to me,' Phillips said. 'I don't know of the case.'

'Then I suggest you look it up,' Laurie said haughtily.

Toby had an inner smile at that. Despite pork, apple sauce, and profiteroles, Laurie was angry again. No-one could fail to admire her spirit.

'My father was innocent, and I'm determined to clear his name. It was when I was delving into my father's, er, problems, that I heard about the missing curate.' She thought for a moment.

'It was Sally, Toby's housekeeper, who first mentioned the man to me. She was telling me about the burglary at the Hall. She said it had been a terrible time in the village, what with the curate disappearing and then the burglary and the death of Mr Edward.'

She paused.

'I asked my father about him, and he remembered that one night, before the curate disappeared, Mr Edward had said he was worried about him. When my father asked what he meant, Mr Edward muttered something about the curate being depressed.'

'So your father believed he was depressed enough to commit suicide?'

There was something in the policeman's tone that Toby didn't much care for.

'My father didn't believe anything. I'm simply telling you what he told me. Mr Edward, Toby's father, believed him to be depressed but, as he's no longer with us, he can't confirm it, can he? However, as the poor man's body has been found in the lake, it seems as if Mr Edward was right. Happy people don't throw themselves in lakes, do they?'

'They don't,' Phillips agreed. 'However, we don't believe Mr Watson threw himself in the lake, as you put it.'

'So what do you believe?' Toby's dislike of this man was increasing by the minute.

'Our forensic team is still carrying out tests,' Phillips explained, 'but we have reason to believe that Mr Watson was murdered.'

A shocked silence met his words. Toby saw the way Laurie's hand flew to her chest, as if she was trying to slow her heartbeat.

'Murdered?' Her voice was little more than a whisper.

'Yes.'

Toby was at a loss for words.

'Reason to believe' meant they were almost certain. Who on earth would murder a curate?

'You seem surprised, Mrs Summerfield,' the younger detective said.

That was putting it mildly, Toby thought.

'I am, yes. When I heard the curate had gone missing, I thought he might have had something to do with the burglary here. Someone framed my father, and I thought it might have been the curate. I imagined he'd faked his disappearance, returned to steal the jewels and then framed my father.'

She let out her breath on a long sigh.

'Obviously not.'

Toby didn't know what to make of it. He cared for Laurie, cared for her deeply, but no-one, not even Laurie herself, could have convinced him that her father was innocent. Now, he had doubts.

It was all too coincidental. If Jim Whitney had confessed to the crime, he would presumably have served a shorter sentence.

That the man loved his daughter, Toby had no doubt. So wouldn't he have confessed so that he might spend more time with her? And now, a murder had been committed here at Kingsley Hall.

'When you look at my father's case,' Laurie said, 'you'll find that the police believe Mr Edward disturbed the thief and paid the price. My father, however, believes that it was murder made to look like a burglary gone wrong.'

'It would seem to me,' Toby said at last,

'there's every possibility that the death of my father and the death of this curate, Mr Watson, could be linked. As Mr Watson's death occurred at around the same time, and as the police clearly didn't know that he'd been murdered, it does make me wonder what else they missed.

'Presumably, I can ask for a new investigation into the death of my father?'

At that, the two detectives were on their feet.

'We'll make enquiries,' Detective Superintendent Phillips promised. 'Meanwhile, I'd like to talk to your housekeeper, if I may.'

'Yes, of course...'

Toby escorted them to the kitchen and left them to talk to Sally. His housekeeper was more than happy to tell them all she remembered of Mr Alan Watson.

Laurie was just going out of the door when he came back to the hall. He caught up with her in the rose garden, and she stood glaring at him.

'Why did you ask for a new investigation?'

'Because I don't like that chap's attitude,' Toby said, 'and because I think this raises questions.'

Surely it simply wasn't possible that they'd sent an innocent man to prison? Even twenty years ago, the police had been well equipped to gather sufficient evidence, Toby thought.

Then he looked at Laurie, and his heart melted.

'Nothing would make me happier than to know your father was innocent.'

She gave him a weary smile.

'Perhaps,' she said, 'but I expect, like the rest of the world, you'll go to your grave not knowing the man my father really is.' She turned, but then changed her mind, and faced him again.

'Oh, and I'd better tell you how I've been spending my salary. I've employed a private investigator.'

'To do what?'

'To see what she can find out.'

'She?'

'Yes. My father told the police that, a few days before your father was killed, a man claiming to be a fine art expert called at the Hall saying he had an appointment with your father. Your father knew nothing about an appointment. Of course, this so-called expert didn't exist, and the police assumed my father was making it all up to save his own skin. Terri, the private investigator, found out that a man using the same name booked into a nearby hotel at around the same time. But I'm sure you're not interested.'

She walked off across the park, leaving him alone with his thoughts. Very disturbing they were, too.

When Dave had told him of the shocking

discovery, he had hoped and prayed with every fibre of his being that it was anyone other than her. Because, although it seemed utter madness, and disloyal to his father's memory, he still had a dream. He wanted her with him, here at Kingsley Hall, for the rest of their days.

Jim Whitney had eaten a light lunch of which the dietician at the hospital would have approved wholeheartedly. He had also taken the fourth tablet of the day. And then the police arrived.

There were two of them, detective sergeants, male and female. He wasn't surprised to see them.

'You'd better come in,' he said.

Laurie hadn't told him about the discovery at Kingsley Hall; he'd seen it on the television. He'd phoned her about it, shortly after she had discovered that the police had identified Alan Watson.

'So it looks as if they'll be re-opening the case, Dad,' she'd said, and she'd sounded so optimistic... Jim wished he could share her optimism.

Laurie, despite what had happened in the past, thought the police would find the missing evidence, arrest the real culprit and clear her dad's name. In her eyes, it was that simple.

'Would you be so kind as to tell us all you

know about Alan Watson?' the male detective sergeant asked.

'I know he was curate at Kingsley for about a year, and then he vanished,' Jim said. 'I remember the woods around the Hall being searched, but nothing was found.'

'Did you know the man?'

'Not really. Enough to pass the time of day with him, but nothing more than that.'

'And when you passed the time of day, how did Mr Watson appear? Happy? Relaxed? Worried? Depressed?'

'He seemed relaxed enough,' Jim said. 'However, and I know my daughter's already told your lot this, my employer, Edward Davis, told me that he was worried about Mr Watson. When I questioned him, he dismissed it.

'I asked him about it again another day, and, although he dismissed it again, he murmured something about the man being depressed.'

'I see.'

All Jim could do was answer their questions as fully and as honestly as he knew how. However, as he looked at the detective sergeant, he knew his worst fears were about to be confirmed. He could see it in the man's eyes.

James Albert Whitney was, once again, chief suspect.

CHAPTER EIGHT

'Will you let me do most of the talking?' Laurie stopped her car outside her dad's flat and turned to Terri.

'Of course. Now stop worrying. It'll be fine.' Terri grabbed her handbag and reached across for her jacket. 'Come on, then. I can't wait to meet your father.'

No sooner were they out of the car than Jim Whitney opened his door wide. Laurie ran to hurl herself into his arms.

'Anyone would think you were pleased to see me,' he said, laughing as he held her tight.

Laurie pulled back to look at him.

'You're looking really well, Dad.'

Remembering her manners, she introduced him to Terri.

It was a huge relief to see Dad looking so well. Ever since he'd phoned to tell her the police had been hounding him – her word, not his – she'd been worried sick about him.

She'd even made a call to Detective Superintendent Phillips.

'He's only just out of hospital after a heart attack,' she'd cried, 'and now you've sent your people to accuse him of–'

'We've accused your father of nothing,' Detective Superintendent Phillips had said patiently.

'I bet he's a suspect,' Laurie said.

'We need to eliminate him.'

Anyway, her dad looked fine. No, better than fine.

'You really do look well, Dad.'

'I am well. I rattle when I move, but apart from that–'

'Oh, shut up!'

'Are we ready then?' he asked, looking from Terri to Laurie.

'I am,' Terri said.

'Me, too.' Surprisingly, Laurie realised she was starving.

When she'd called her dad to tell him she was planning a flying visit at the weekend – and bringing a private investigator with her – he hadn't flinched.

'Lovely! I'll take you both to dinner. My treat,' he'd said. 'I still get my staff discount.'

At the time, Laurie had been convinced she wouldn't be able to eat a thing, but seeing her dad laughing and joking, she was ravenous.

By the time they arrived at the hotel where Jim worked, the dining-room was already busy. For all that, the welcome they received brought the sting of tears to Laurie's eyes.

Her dad was well-liked and respected wherever he went. Why couldn't the police see that? Why couldn't Toby?

She pushed that final question away. Thinking of Toby was strictly off limits this weekend.

'What a lovely place,' Terri was saying. 'When you told me it was a family business, Laurie, I was expecting something much smaller – a dozen bedrooms at most!'

'There are sixty bedrooms,' Jim explained. 'And the food is excellent. The chef's French, and he's a perfectionist.' He looked around the busy room. 'People still like the personal touch, and that's what they get here.'

Their table was next to a huge window overlooking lawns that sloped gently down to the golf course. It was the perfect setting.

Midway through their main course, Laurie's appetite had dulled sufficiently for her to concentrate on more important matters.

'So tell me again,' she insisted. 'What exactly did the police have to say?'

'I'm surprised they didn't take you in for questioning,' Terri put in.

'I thought they were going to,' Jim said, frowning slightly. 'I expect they thought it was more trouble than it was worth. They've got nothing on me, and would have had to let me go.

'I might be chief suspect, but only because they consider me capable of murder. They need more than that. A lot more.'

Terri nodded.

'They asked me all I knew about the curate, Alan Watson,' he told them, 'and that wasn't a lot. I barely remember him. It was so long ago.'

'What about the man who claimed he was a fine arts expert?' Terri asked. 'Can you remember anything about him?'

'Charles Taylor? Oh, yes. If he walked in here now, looking as he did twenty years ago, I'd recognise him immediately.'

Laurie and Terri exchanged glances, surprised by his confidence.

'He looked nothing like a fine arts dealer,' Jim went on. 'He was pushy to the point of rudeness. Instead of leaving when I said Mr Edward was away, he did his utmost to get inside. The pushier he became, the firmer I was – I suppose that's why I remember him so well.'

Terri rummaged through her handbag for her recorder and switched it on.

'What did he look like?' she asked.

'He was a big man – tall and broad – with dark hair slicked back. His hair was longer than it should have been, and it curled over his collar. He wore dark-rimmed glasses. If Mr Edward had been planning to part with any paintings, he would have approached one of the top firms. This chap, Charles Taylor, didn't look as if he came from one of those places. He wore a dark suit that was a little too small for him and it had gone shiny at the elbows. White shirt. Tie. He had a ruddy complexion, I remember. Oh, and he wore a huge, square gold ring on the middle finger of his left hand.'

He looked at their shocked faces.

'That's about it.'

'You remember all that?' Terri said in amazement.

'I do.' Jim nodded. 'The day he called, I thought he was an odd character. Then, when Mr Edward told me he'd never heard of the chap, I was suspicious. Hindsight's a wonderful thing, of course. I forgot about him until the burglary at the Hall.'

'And the police couldn't trace him from your description?' Terri was appalled. 'I discovered that he'd checked – well, someone using that name had checked into a hotel in Burnley. And that's twenty years later.'

'Ah,' Jim said, 'but you believed someone using that name existed. The police thought I'd invented him.'

Already, her dad and Terri were friends. Laurie was pleased.

'I'm not sure he was responsible, though,' Jim went on thoughtfully. 'I didn't let him put a foot inside the Hall, so he couldn't have known where the safe was.'

'It's all a bit coincidental, though,' Laurie pointed out.

'Very,' Terri agreed.

Terri had lots more questions, and Jim answered as fully as he could, but by the time they'd finished their meal, they were no further forward.

Laurie was surprised Dad seemed so optimistic about it all. It was as if he believed that just because new questions were being asked, new answers would come to light.

She sincerely hoped he was right.

'So are you staying at the Hall?' Dad asked her.

'For the time being, yes. Toby was insistent.'

She either carried on with her job and hoped that by being on the spot, as it were, she would be able to unearth some clues, or she allowed her pride to win, told Toby exactly what she thought of people who believed her father to be a thief, and a killer, and returned to Middlesex.

For the time being, it was better to stay in Lancashire.

On Monday, Laurie was in the library at Kingsley Hall, looking through the old books Toby had unpacked. There were hundreds, and according to Toby, there were still a lot more in store.

'Nice to see this lot back where they belong,' Sally said as she came in. 'They take a lot of dusting, mind.'

That was one job Laurie wouldn't like.

'There are a lot more still to come, I imagine,' Sally went on. 'Mr Edward collected books like some people collect stamps. He read a lot, granted, but no-one could read this much!'

Laurie had to smile. She had been hoping to find something on the original gardens at the Hall but, so far, she'd had no luck.

'I still keep thinking about that poor curate,' Sally went on with a sigh. 'Can't get the man out of my mind at all. Such a nice young fellow he was.'

Laurie nodded sympathetically.

'It's obvious he had problems, though,' Sally went on. 'I remember him coming here once, not long before he vanished. He came to see Mr Edward, and he looked as if he had the problems of the world on his shoulders. Funny, now I come to think of it.' She sat down at the large table. 'I remember him coming round. When I told him Mr Edward wasn't here, there was no budging him. He would have waited a week if necessary, I think.'

'And where was Mr Edward?'

'I can't remember,' Sally said. 'Your dad had taken him somewhere. Anyway, they weren't far away – young Alan only had an hour or so to wait. He wouldn't have a cup of tea or anything while he waited. He simply sat in the drawing-room, looking as if the devil himself were after him.'

'Really?' Laurie was intrigued. 'So why did he want to see Toby's dad so urgently?'

'I never knew. They talked for a long time, probably a couple of hours, and when Alan Watson left, Mr Edward looked as worried as he did.'

So Mr Edward had told her dad he was worried about the curate!

Laurie's mind raced with questions. Alan Watson must have been in serious trouble – enough trouble to cost him his life. If a curate were in such trouble, wouldn't he confide in the vicar? Surely Mr Casper must know what problems the curate had...

'How soon after that did he go missing?' Laurie asked.

'Ah, well, that's difficult to answer,' Sally told her. 'You see, he set off for a fortnight's holiday, going home to his parents. They lived in Scotland. Except, it must have been a spur of the moment decision,' she added, 'because they knew nothing about it. When they came down here, saying they hadn't heard from him for some time, well – that's when folk started looking for him.'

'Dad says he remembers them searching the woods,' Laurie put in.

'That's right. And it wasn't long after that poor Mr Edward met his maker.'

'A month, wasn't it?'

'About that. Maybe less.' She thought for

a moment. 'I think it would have been less than that. You see, we all thought the young curate was in Scotland…'

That afternoon, working in the grounds, Laurie thought over the things Sally had told her. If only Toby's father was here to tell them about that meeting he had with Alan Watson!

Odd that the curate should take his troubles to Mr Edward , though. Odd, too, to tell everyone he was going back to Scotland to visit his parents.

She was so deep in thought that when Toby's dog raced up, she was almost knocked off her feet.

'Holly, you gave me the fright of my life!'

Toby soon caught up.

'Is this dog being a nuisance?'

'No.' Laughing, Laurie fondled the dog's ears. 'She's fine. I was miles away, and she made me jump, that's all.'

Laurie had worried that Holly might damage the new young plants, but, although she raced about at speed, she'd done no damage at all. Yet.

'So,' Toby said, 'did you have a good weekend?'

Laurie always felt uncomfortable when discussing her father. It was ridiculous, but it couldn't be helped.

'Yes, very nice, thanks.'

'Good. And your father's well?'

'He is. Yes.'

'Good.'

It seemed that Toby was equally uncomfortable.

'Did you find what you wanted among those books?' he asked, changing the subject.

'Not yet.' She had to smile. 'I had no idea there were so many.'

'There are lots more. They've been in store for so long that I've forgotten what's there.' Toby rubbed a thoughtful finger across his chin. 'I've also been speaking to my aunt this morning. When my father was killed, I was given his journals.'

Laurie's interest was caught.

'Your father kept a journal?'

'Yes. I haven't seen them since I was – oh, I must have been about eighteen. Don't get excited, though. As far as I can remember, they were very businesslike – a lot of boring entries connected with the running of the estate. Oh, and his handwriting was appalling.'

She smiled, but it must be difficult for Toby to sort through his father's things.

'Anyway, as far as my aunt can remember,' he went on, 'the journals were put in store with the books. I'm going to have another look through, and see if I come across them. As I said, they didn't seem of interest at the time.'

Laurie didn't quite know what to say. She would give a lot to read through his father's journals, but she knew she couldn't ask.

They both turned to watch a lorry coming slowly up the drive.

'That's the gravel for the back driveway,' Laurie said. 'At least, I hope it is.'

They walked towards the house and, sure enough, it was the delivery of gravel. Laurie directed the driver around the back of the Hall, and assured him that Dave and the rest of the gang were waiting for him.

'How far behind schedule are we?' Toby asked, as the lorry drove away in a cloud of dust.

'Not too far, considering. And everyone's willing to work overtime. It'll be fine. You'll be able to open in the spring.'

'You'll be here for that, won't you?'

The question surprised Laurie. At least, the hesitant way in which it was asked surprised her.

How different things would have been, she thought, if this had been just another job. If she'd met Toby as a stranger, nothing more than her employer–

Still, it was pointless dwelling on that.

'You'll want to see the project through, won't you?' he persisted.

'I'd like to, yes,' she said. 'It's just that–'

'Then you will,' he said firmly, cutting her off. 'The rest of it–'

He broke off as they heard another vehicle, and turned to see a car coming along the drive.

'Police,' Toby muttered grimly.

'They always seem to bring bad news,' Laurie said. 'I've started to dread their visits.'

There was a woman in the car but she didn't get out.

'Detective Sergeant McGrath,' Toby greeted the policeman.

'Just a quick courtesy call. We've traced your elusive Charles Taylor.'

'The man who called at the Hall?' Laurie hardly dared to believe it. 'The man who claimed to be a fine arts dealer?'

'The very same,' he replied.

'What does he have to do with the death of the curate?' Toby asked quickly.

'Nothing, as far as we know. As his name was mentioned, however, we ran it through the computer. He's used that alias three times to our knowledge.'

'Twenty years ago,' Laurie pointed out, 'the police said my father had invented the man.'

'It has no bearing on your father's case,' Detective Sergeant McGrath said.

'What makes you so sure?' Toby asked. 'It seems to me now that serious errors were made when my father's death was investigated.'

'I don't think so,' the sergeant replied. 'Charles Taylor is an alias used by Victor Smith, a petty criminal who's currently serving eighteen months for burglary.'

'What he's doing now is irrelevant, isn't it?' Toby said.

'Perhaps,' the detective agreed. 'But he's a petty criminal who's spent a lot of time in prison, and on the night your father was killed, he was in police custody.'

Laurie's spirits sank. So Charles Taylor – or Victor Smith – had nothing to do with it. There could be no better alibi.

'You've spoken to the man?' Toby asked.

'We've spoken to him, and several others, regarding the murder of Mr Alan Watson, yes.'

Terri had warned Laurie how reluctant the police would be to discuss her dad's case. Unless substantial new evidence came to light, they wanted that file to remain closed.

'And you don't think the death of my father and the death of the curate could be linked?'

'No, sir, we don't,' Detective Sergeant Mc-Grath said firmly. 'Victor Smith did admit to calling at the hall in November, 1985. However, because he wasn't allowed inside–'

'Because my father wouldn't allow it!' Laurie burst out, and the sergeant looked at her.

'He's an opportunist, nothing more. And as I said, on the night in question, he was in police custody.'

'How very convenient,' Toby murmured.

'Now, may I raise a couple of points? Let us assume that James Whitney, the man employed and trusted by my father for eighteen years, is innocent.'

Laurie looked at Toby in amazement, but it was impossible to read his face. Did he believe that, finally? It was difficult to know. He did, however, look like a man determined to get the truth – no matter what the cost.

'There's no evidence to suggest that Mr Whitney invented Charles Taylor's call at the Hall one day. The police, in their wisdom, decided he was lying. We now know that wasn't the case. Mr Whitney also claimed that he had no idea who sent him the bundle of cash. Again, the police decided he was lying. Do we assume they got that wrong, too? Do we assume that the events of that November night in 1985 happened exactly as Mr Whitney described them?'

It took all Laurie's resolve not to throw her arms around Toby and hug him. He must believe it!

'We assume that the investigating officers and the jury involved reached the right decision,' the sergeant said.

'And if they didn't?'

'I'm sure they did.' Clearly unwilling to discuss it further, the detective began walking back to his car.

'We'll be in touch,' he called as he climbed inside.

They watched until the car was out of sight.

'Do you really believe my father could be innocent?' Laurie had to know.

'Laurie, I no longer know what to believe. I came back to the Hall resolved to make it my home again, determined to put the past behind me. Since then–' He shook his head. 'The past seems determined to haunt me.'

Her heart like a lead weight, Laurie made to turn away, but Toby was too quick for her. He took her arm.

'I know the past haunts you, too,' he said gently, his fingers on her wrist. 'For all our sakes, we need to know the truth.'

'Yes,' she agreed.

'And I'm determined that we will know the truth,' he added.

Three days later, Toby was sitting in the library with his father's journals on the table in front of him.

He didn't know what he was looking for, or what he hoped to find. He only knew that they needed the truth.

He walked over to the window and gazed out. Laurie and Dave were moving large urns around in what would soon be the rose garden. Laurie was viewing the tall urns from all angles and, as he watched, she threw back her head and laughed at something Dave said.

Toby's biggest worry was what the truth might do to Laurie. If her father was proved innocent, fine. But what if he wasn't? What would that do to her?

He couldn't help wondering what his own father would have made of this. He'd been an uncomplicated, genuine, gentle person, content to live a quiet life here at the Hall. He would have hated this mystery.

Toby returned to his seat, and with a heavy sigh, he opened the last journal.

His father's handwriting was appalling, and he often used abbreviations. Why shouldn't he? After all, the entries hadn't been written with readers in mind.

His father's last entry was an involved account of repairs needed at the gatehouse, the cottage Laurie now had.

Difficult appointment Armstrong 2 p.m. A (squiggle) man?

Try as he might, Toby couldn't decipher that squiggle. A what man?

Armstrong was presumably the Kingsley lawyer at the time, but why would an appointment with him be difficult? As far as Toby knew, his father had never used his services.

Then he saw Alan Watson's name.

Long discussion with young Alan Watson regarding (squiggle). Very concerned.

When Sally came into the room, Toby was glad to give his eyes a rest.

'I wondered where you'd got to,' his housekeeper said. 'You haven't appeared for your afternoon cuppa. I'll bring one along here, shall I?'

Toby smiled inwardly. All these years on and Sally still insisted on mothering him.

'Please, Sally.'

Ten minutes later, a tray laden with tea and biscuits was placed in front of him.

'Thank you.'

'Is that Mr Edward's writing?' Sally nodded at the open journal.

'It is, yes,' Toby replied. 'I don't suppose you can decipher it, can you, Sally?'

She chuckled.

'Dear me, I had enough practice! So did young Laurie's dad. Mr Edward was a great one for leaving notes for people. Many's the time me and Jim Whitney tried to carry out your father's instructions from those notes.'

Toby turned the pages until he came to the final entry.

'Here,' he said. 'What do you make of that?'

'Difficult appointment Armstrong 2 p.m. A dangerous man?'

'Dangerous? Are you sure?'

'As sure as I can be with Mr Edward's writing, yes.'

Toby leaned back in his chair.

'What on earth can he mean?'

'I can well believe him not wanting to keep an appointment with Armstrong. Your father never liked him.'

'Really?'

'Oh, yes. That Daniel Armstrong was un-popular with a lot of people. It was unlike your father to take a dislike to someone, too.'

A dangerous man?

Toby's mind was racing. On the day his father was killed, he'd kept an appointment with a man he considered dangerous.

'What about this, Sally?' Toby quickly thumbed back through the pages until he reached the entry regarding Alan Watson. 'What does that say?'

'*Long discussion—*' Sally paused to concentrate on each word. '*Long discussion with Alan Watson* – that'll be the poor curate – *regarding Ivy Bleasdon. Very concerned.*'

'Are you sure?'

'Fairly,' she said, nodding.

'Who's Ivy Bleasdon, do you know?' Toby would like a chat with her, whoever she was.

'She used to live in that cottage at the back of the school – before the village school closed. A nice old lady. She died years ago.' Sally thought for a moment. 'She probably died the same year as your father, now I come to think of it.'

That, of course, was always going to be the problem. Twenty years was a long time...

'Now Ivy was a fan of Daniel Armstrong,' Sally went on with a wry smile. 'Give him his due, though, he was good to her. Sorted out all her finances, her will – that sort of stuff. The only family Ivy had was a daughter in Australia, and as she had no-one else, she left everything – her house and a tidy sum, I believe – to him, to Daniel Armstrong.'

'Did she?' Toby said thoughtfully.'

'Died quite suddenly, if I remember rightly,' Sally murmured. 'Anyway, I must get on. I've got pies in the oven...'

When six o'clock arrived that evening, Toby could stand it no more.

'Come on, Holly,' he said, rising to his feet. 'Let's get some fresh air.'

It was another lovely evening, still pleasantly warm. Toby set off with the dog running at his heels, and headed for the hills. It did nothing to clear his mind. So many questions and so many names raced around his head.

Jim Whitney – guilty or innocent? Alan Watson – was his murder connected to the burglary at the Hall?

Daniel Armstrong – what had been said at that 2 p.m. appointment? Ivy Bleasdon – why had his father been concerned about her?

Two things had happened at Kingsley Hall. A young curate had been murdered and his body had been disposed of in the lake. Shortly afterwards, a burglar had broken into Kingsley Hall, stolen jewels, killed Toby's father, presumably panicked and thrown the jewels in the well.

Could the two be connected? Or was Toby reading something into nothing?

He was surprised to see someone ahead of him. He rarely met anyone out here. She turned, and he was even more surprised to see that it was Laurie.

Where did she find her energy? After a long day working at the Hall, Toby would have expected her to be sitting at home with her feet up.

She spotted him, seemed to hesitate, and then began walking towards him.

'Great minds think alike,' she said, smiling. 'Isn't it a gorgeous evening?'

'It is.'

'I was remembering riding the ponies over these hills,' she said softly. 'Do you remember Merry? She'd go so far, and then she'd want to head back to the stables.'

Toby smiled. He'd forgotten about Merry's foibles.

'I remember how long it took to coax her within a hundred yards of a horsebox.'

'Oh, yes.' Laurie spluttered with laughter.

How could he accept that Jim Whitney was guilty, Toby wondered, when he loved the man's daughter with every breath in his body?

'I've been looking at my father's journal.' He pushed the thought aside.

'And?' she pressed.

'I don't know,' he admitted. 'Come with me and see for yourself…'

They walked back to the Hall. Conversation was mundane. How could they recall the happy memories when the events of that November night would for ever come between them?

It was chilly in the library now but Laurie didn't seem to notice.

'I did warn you about my father's handwriting,' Toby reminded her.

Although she smiled and nodded, she appeared almost afraid to look as Toby opened it to his father's last entry.

'I don't suppose you can read that,' he said, pointing to the relevant line.

'*Difficult appointment Armstrong 2 p.m.,*' she read. '*A dangerous man?*'

'Dangerous,' Toby repeated. 'Yes, that's what Sally thought.'

'What did he mean by that?'

'I don't know.' Toby looked at her and his decision was made.

'I'm going to call the police,' he said briskly. 'On the day my father died, he kept an appointment with a man he considered to be dangerous. I think that's reason enough to reopen the case.'

'The police won't agree,' she warned him.

'Then I'll tell them I'll be in touch with my contacts at the Home Office.'

She looked impressed.

'Do you have contacts at the Home Office?'

'None that spring to mind, but I'm sure my uncle does.'

A dozen emotions flickered across her face, but uppermost was a mix of hope and despair.

'They'll probably accuse my dad of forging entries in your father's journal,' she said, and, if he wasn't mistaken, a shimmer of tears was visible.

'Laurie, no.' He reached for her hand and held it tight. 'No-one could copy my father's handwriting. It's appalling!'

She smiled, but the despair was still visible.

Toby longed to take her in his arms, tell her he loved her, and kiss away her troubles. He reached for the phone instead.

CHAPTER NINE

If looks could have killed, Toby would have met his Maker the moment he opened the door to Superintendent Phillips.

'Mr Davis, I believe you have some paperwork for me to see?'

Toby led him to the study.

'Are there any other papers, letters – anything else belonging to your father?' Superintendent Phillips gazed at Edward's papers, spread out on the table.

'Just his journals,' Toby explained. 'My father was something of a hoarder, so there are some letters here, mainly connected to the running of the estate, so I don't think there's anything relevant. You're welcome to examine them, of course.'

'We'll take them with us,' the detective said, in a resigned sort of way. 'And we'll need to make sure the journal is authentic.'

'Meaning?' Toby asked.

The detective shrugged.

'Ah, I see,' Toby said, understanding dawning. 'You think I might have written the entries myself? Why would I do that? All I want is the truth.'

'Yes, I'm sure you do. We all do.'

'Then we're all happy,' Toby said briskly, knowing that the Superintendent was far from happy.

'Most of us already know the truth,' the policeman added.

'That Jim Whitney killed my father? Maybe.'

The detective shrugged again.

Toby sympathised with him. One thing was certain, without his uncle's friendship with the chief constable, the case wouldn't have been reopened.

'You have to admit it's odd,' Toby insisted.

'My father keeps an appointment with a man he considers dangerous, and within twenty-four hours, he's dead?'

'Daniel Armstrong had lived in Kingsley for some time. He was a well-respected professional, and no doubt he and your father met often.' The policeman was polite, but firm.

'Do you have any fresh leads on the death of Alan Watson, the curate?' Toby asked.

'Not at the moment, no,' Superintendent Phillips admitted. 'And having to look at other things – like the tragic death of your father – will take up time that could be used on that case.'

'Yes, but I'm sure the time won't be wasted.'

'Are you? Can't you imagine how greedy a butler might get? When a man spends eighteen years of his life seeing how the other half live, waiting on his master hand and foot – well, it's human nature to want something more for yourself.'

'Maybe,' Toby said. But there were too many unanswered questions for his liking.

Of course, it might just be wishful thinking on his part, because he didn't want Jim Whitney to be a thief and a killer.

For one thing, Toby was in love with the man's daughter.

For another, he'd always considered his own father a good judge of character. Toby didn't want to acknowledge that his father had made a foolish choice in Jim Whitney.

But what about the man himself? If Jim really was innocent, he'd lost twelve years of his life behind bars. Society would have treated him as a criminal ever since.

'Jim Whitney has always protested his innocence,' Toby reminded the detective. 'Why would he bother? He's served his time, paid the price.'

'Guilt,' Phillips answered confidently. 'I'm sure he didn't intend to kill your father. All he wanted was to steal the jewels and make a better life for himself.'

He gestured to the pile of papers in front of him.

'Is this the lot?'

'As far as I know, yes. If anything else turns up, I'll let you know.'

Minutes later, Toby was holding a receipt for his father's journals and a collection of old letters.

Jim Whitney was doing as the doctor ordered – and enjoying it. Taking a brisk walk every day was never a chore.

He was about to go home when the familiar sight of his friend Scooby Doo made him smile. Pam wasn't far behind her dog.

It reminded Jim of the day Laurie had first spoken about the job at Kingsley Hall. She'd told him about it as they'd sat on that bench he'd just passed, and Laurie had teased him then about Pam…

What a lot had happened since then.

Jim stroked Scooby Doo, the enormous Great Dane, and walked towards his owner.

'I wondered if we'd see you today,' Pam greeted Jim. 'You're looking well, Jim.'

'I'm feeling well. Do you mind if I do another lap of the park with you?'

Smiling, she shook her head.

'What a silly question. You know perfectly well that I love your company.'

Jim enjoyed Pam's company, too, but he didn't want her getting any romantic ideas.

Besides, Pam had been divorced for fifteen years and Jim gathered she valued her independence.

She was a good friend, though. On his first visit to the park after leaving hospital, he'd been touched and surprised when she said she'd missed him. Since then, he'd felt able to confide in her.

'Anything new?' she asked as they walked.

'Yes,' he said, having to bite back a surge of hope. 'It seems they've reopened my case.'

'Really? But that's wonderful.' Her delight touched him.

'It's little short of a miracle,' he told her with a wry smile. 'It seems as if it's a matter of who you know rather than what you know. Apparently, Toby's uncle has contacts in high places. He's also friends with the chief constable.'

'So this is Toby's doing!'

That pleased Jim almost as much as the case being reopened.

'There's no new evidence that I'm aware of,' he added quickly, not wanting to raise her hopes, either. 'Other than the entry in Mr Edward's journal–'

'His appointment with the dangerous man,' Pam murmured.

'Daniel Armstrong. But there, it's probably nothing.' At the moment, Jim was on a see-saw of hope and despair. 'But it's good to know that Toby's giving me a chance.'

'If my father had been killed, I'd demand the truth, too.'

'Would you?' Jim asked doubtfully. 'Or would you accept the verdict of the police and the jury?'

She thought for a moment.

'I suppose it's difficult to say. But if I had the slightest doubt, I'd want the truth. It must be awful not knowing. There's no real closure, is there?'

They walked on past the lake.

'What about Laurie?' Pam asked. 'Do you still believe she's falling for Toby?'

'I think she's fallen. When I was in hospital, I could tell she had feelings for him. It must be difficult for them both. Laurie is fiercely proud of her old dad, and–'

'Quite rightly!'

Jim laughed.

'I don't know about that. But the man she fancies has spent most of his life believing that her dad's a cheat – and a killer.'

'Mm. Would you be pleased if they got together?'

'I've asked myself that so many times.' Jim paused. 'All I want is Laurie's happiness. If Toby could make her happy then I'd be delighted.'

'You're very fond of her ex-husband, though, aren't you? Do you think – hope – they might get back together?' Pam patted his arm. 'Sorry, I'm being nosy. Tell me to mind my own business.'

'Not at all. It's good to talk things over.'

It made a refreshing change to get a woman's view on things, too. Micky was marvellous, the best friend a man could have, but Pam often saw things differently.

Her hand was still on his arm, he noticed.

'I do like Steve,' he said, trying not to think about how good it was to feel her touch. 'But I've given up all hope of them getting back together. They're great friends, and I'm sure they always will be, but there's no–' He paused, searching for the right word.

'Spark?' Pam suggested.

'Exactly. There's no spark.'

It was uncanny the way Pam often put words into his mouth. Uncanny how they shared the same views on so many things...

At the entrance to the park, Jim began saying cheerio.

'Why not come round to my place one evening?' Pam asked suddenly. 'I love cooking and it would be a rare treat to cook for two.'

'Well, it's very kind of you, Pam, but–' Jim had visions of a small table set for two adorned with red candles. The thought was horrifying.

'Jim, I'm like you. I'm set in my ways. No way am I looking for a relationship!' She laughed suddenly. 'You've no need to worry. I don't have designs on you. I simply thought it would make a pleasant change – for both of us.'

'In that case, I accept. Thank you, Pam.'

'My pleasure. You can do the washing-up.' And she strode off with Scooby Doo.

Laurie knew she would never be able to repay Toby's kindness. Thanks to him, her dad's case was being looked into again. Even if nothing came of it, she would always be grateful to him for that.

More than that, she would always be grateful to him for considering that her dad just might be innocent. To her, it was obvious, but she knew that Toby had spent most of his life believing him guilty.

Now he was buying her and Terri lunch.

'I assume you're starving, Laurie?' He

handed them each a menu.

'You assume right! It's six hours since I had breakfast and I'm almost passing out from hunger.'

'What about you, Terri?' he asked, and she grinned.

'Getting hungrier by the second,' she said, running her finger down the menu.

It didn't take them long to order. Conversation, not surprisingly, soon took a more serious turn.

'Is your husband working on this case?' Toby asked Terri. 'I know he's a detective.'

'Sadly, he isn't, so there's not much he can tell me. They have confirmed that your father's journal is authentic, though.'

'I could have told them that!' Toby said dryly.

'I'd love to know why your father thought the lawyer a dangerous man, Toby.'

'Tell me again about the woman your father mentioned in his journal,' Terri said, as the food arrived. 'Ivy Bleasdon, was it?'

'Yes, but I'm afraid there's nothing much to tell. My father simply wrote that he was very concerned about her.'

'The really odd thing is that she was already dead when Toby's dad wrote that,' Laurie said, frowning. 'She died quite suddenly by all accounts.'

'According to Sally, he attended her funeral,' Toby said.

196

'Kathleen Eve died suddenly, too,' Terri said after a while.

'Did she?' That was news to Laurie. 'That was the one who remembered Daniel Armstrong in her will and not her daughter?

'I thought you said she was old?'

'She was well into her eighties, but it was still sudden.'

'Ivy Bleasdon was eighty, too,' Laurie murmured. 'At least, Sally thinks she was.'

'I'll check that,' Terri said. 'It's odd, isn't it? Two elderly women die suddenly – and both mention Daniel Armstrong in their wills.'

'I don't think that's particularly unusual,' Toby said thoughtfully. 'Elderly people, especially with no families, take a lot of comfort from professionals who help them out. A kindly lawyer would be a Godsend.'

'I suppose so,' Terri agreed grudgingly.

'What about Alan Watson?' Laurie asked. 'Have the police discovered anything there?'

'A lot of blanks, I gather,' Terri told her. 'He was a popular man who had lots of friends, sociable and outgoing, financially OK. No debts. No enemies.' She grimaced.

'Someone clearly took a dislike to him, though. Enough of a dislike to kill him.'

She speared a piece of beef.

'I'd like to know where he was killed,' she went on. 'So would the police, of course. But I can't believe he was killed down where he was found – someone must have taken his body to the lake.

'That's not easy – it's either a difficult walk across fields, or a long walk or drive, in full view of the Hall. Far too risky.'

Laurie shuddered.

'This is cheery talk,' she said, pulling a face.

'Isn't it just?' Terri sighed.

So they spoke of other matters, like the progress being made on the gardens.

'It's wonderful to see it all coming together, isn't it Toby?' Laurie said.

'Very exciting.' The expression in his eyes caused her heart to skip a few beats. His thoughtful gaze rested on her for so long that she was almost pleased when he began talking about Alan Watson again.

'He wasn't married, was he?' he asked Terri.

'No, no girlfriend, either.'

'What about his parents?'

'Both still alive, and still living in the same house they were then.'

'In Scotland?'

'That's right. They run a bookshop, I gather.'

Once again, they forced themselves to discuss other things – like how Toby would cope with hundreds of people tramping across his property every day.

'I shall console myself with the knowledge that they're paying to keep me in my home,' he said. 'That's always assuming there are hundreds of people. If no-one turns up, I'll be looking for a cardboard box to rent.'

'They'll come in droves,' Laurie told him, laughing at his worried frown.

On Wednesday evening, after a long and tiring day, Laurie was about to enjoy a leisurely soak in the bath when Toby arrived at the cottage.

'Come in. Is everything all right?'

'Yes. Yes, fine.'

As always, she was struck by how small the house was when Toby was inside it. Her home suited her perfectly. Being small meant less to clean, but it seemed to shrink with Toby dominating the rooms.

'I've been thinking.'

'Oh.'

'About Alan Watson. I can't help thinking that he's connected with what happened to my father. I know there appears to be nothing linking the two but–'

'I know what you mean.' Laurie wondered what he was getting at. 'Nothing happens in Kingsley for generations and then, within the space of a month or so, a young curate is murdered and your father is killed, during what was – or what was made to look like – a burglary. It's all too coincidental.'

'Exactly,' Toby agreed.

Laurie still had no idea what he was getting at. She'd thought all along that the curate had to be involved. At one point, he'd been her chief suspect for the burglary at the Hall.

Even on finding out that the poor chap had been murdered, she'd still thought he must be part of the jigsaw.

'How do you feel about a trip to Scotland?' Toby took her completely by surprise.

'Scotland?'

'Yes. Alan Watson's parents are easy enough to find. We could talk to them, and possibly other people who knew him.'

Immediately, Laurie had visions of Alan Watson's family and friends solving the riddle for them. But...

'The police have already spoken to them,' she pointed out. 'They had to when they identified his body.'

'I know, but I still think it's worth a try.' He stood with his arms folded, a frown on his face. 'His body was found on my land, and I think it would be a nice gesture to offer my condolences.

'Besides, people will often talk more freely when the police aren't firing questions at them.'

'It's a thought,' Laurie said slowly.

'I'm going,' Toby said, as if he just had made up his mind. 'Will you come with me? You can spare two or three days, can't you?'

'I'll have to check with my boss,' she said.

'Your boss would give you the moon if he could, and you know it.'

Laurie didn't know how to respond to that. The lighthearted remark brought a rush of colour to her face and made her throat dry.

As she gazed at him, she wondered how she would feel about Toby Davis if he were a stranger. If her family hadn't been banished from the Hall in disgrace, if Toby hadn't spent most of his life believing her dad capable of killing his–

But that stood between them and it always would. There was no point wondering how she might have felt about Toby.

'Would you like a coffee?' she asked briskly.

'Some other time.' He looked at his watch. 'I have a visitor arriving any minute, so I'd better get back to the Hall. We'll go to Scotland on Friday, shall we? Have the weekend there?'

'Yes, OK.'

'We could fly, but I think it will be better to drive. Easy enough to hire a car, I suppose, but then you have the hassle of collecting and returning it. We'll drive, shall we?'

'That would probably be best,' she agreed.

'Good. Inverness must be a good seven or eight-hour drive but – well, I'll look into it.'

With that, he left her to her thoughts.

They were so jumbled that she made a coffee and took it out into the garden.

After a day that had been too hot for comfort, the evening was pleasantly warm. Birds that had sheltered from the heat all day were now singing merrily, and bees continued to work their way over the flowers.

Laurie knew that she and Toby had no future. Despite the constant day dreams, that was a fact. There was too much between them.

Given that fact, there was no need whatsoever for her mind to be racing at the thought of going to Scotland with him. Even so…

Where would they stay? There would be meals out. What should she wear? Something casual, because they'd be spending a lot of time in the car…

She was mentally packing her suitcase with clothes that were far from casual when the sound of a vehicle turning into the drive caught her attention.

From her vantage point, she had a good view of the car and the driver. The car was low, red and sporty. Music was blasting out from the radio. The driver had the top down and her long auburn hair was being tossed around by the wind.

That, no doubt, was Toby's visitor.

When the car was out of sight, leaving only a cloud of dust behind it, Laurie thought again of the woman driving the car. She'd be around the same age as Toby, she guess. But

202

who was she?

Toby had lots of friends that Laurie didn't know, obviously, just as she had lots that he didn't know. Laurie didn't have young, attractive friends calling in the evening, though.

Less than an hour later, her bath forgotten and her imagination running wild, Laurie saw Toby's car going down the drive. Sitting beside him in the passenger seat was his visitor.

He must be taking her out to dinner.

Not that Laurie cared. Heavens, it was none of her business what he did in his spare time.

So why was she suddenly in such a bad mood?

Early on Friday morning, Laurie was sitting in that same passenger seat heading for Scotland. The sun was shining, the sky was blue, and she was as excited as a schoolchild on a trip to the seaside.

She liked to watch Toby drive. He was a careful driver, and a confident one. His hands were light on the steering wheel.

'Did you have a good time on Wednesday evening?' she asked, guessing he wasn't going to mention it.

'Sorry?' He had to think. 'Oh, Wednesday. Yes, yes, pleasant, thanks.'

He slowed the car before pulling out to

overtake a lorry.

'I saw your visitor arrive,' Laurie pushed on.

'Right.'

Anyone else, Laurie thought crossly, would offer some explanation, like 'She's my cousin' or 'It was business.' Not that the woman in question looked as if she had anything serious on her mind.

Anyway, it was none of Laurie's business. They drove on.

'Nice car,' Laurie said at last.

'Where?' Toby looked around him.

Was he being deliberately obtuse? Laurie didn't think so.

'The one your visitor was driving.'

'Oh.' And he actually laughed. 'Yes, very nice. An Alfa Romeo Spider.'

Laurie clamped her jaw shut and stared out of the window. Let him have his jokes – and his secrets. She didn't care.

'Thinking about it, you must know Valerie,' he said thoughtfully. 'She and her brother, Charles, often visited the Hall when we were children.'

Valerie and Charles? The names meant nothing to Laurie. Toby had had lots of friends, though.

'And you still keep in touch with them both?'

'Yes. I rarely see Valerie – she's a hot-shot theatre agent – but I see Charles quite often.'

Valerie and Charles…

Memories slowly surfaced – a tall, thin boy with ginger hair building a snowman, and a girl describing everything as tiresome.

'Actually, I think I do remember them. Did Charles have ginger hair – a tall boy about your age?'

'That's him.' Toby nodded. 'His sister, Valerie, was–'

'A snob,' Laurie finished for him as another memory surfaced. 'She couldn't understand why the servants' children were allowed to join the Christmas festivities.'

'Really?' His gaze left the road briefly as he frowned at her. He clearly didn't remember eight-year-old Laurie's reaction to that gem, and Laurie didn't intend to enlighten him.

'So how long will it take to get there?' she asked, eager for a change of subject. 'And what if Alan Watson's parents don't want to speak to us?'

'They do. I spoke to his father on the phone. He and his wife are expecting us at ten o'clock in the morning. I've booked us into a hotel in Inverness for tonight.'

While Toby's car ate up the miles, Laurie tried to get her thoughts in order.

What would they say to Alan Watson's parents? Was it possible that they would be able to shed any light on the events in Kingsley the year their son died?

The hotel in Inverness – would she and

Toby have dinner together? Meet in the bar for a drink? She'd wear the mauve dress she'd brought along – assuming it wasn't too creased. Packing had never been one of her skills.

'You hit her,' Toby said suddenly, and Laurie's heart sank.

'I did,' she admitted.

Young Valerie, visiting the Hall at Christmas, had spent the entire time describing everything as tiresome. The weather, the food, the walk to church – it was all tiresome.

Laurie had been at the end of her tether when Valerie had demanded to know why 'the servant's girl' was allowed to join in the game of charades. At that, Laurie had hit her with a plastic tennis racket.

Toby was suddenly laughing.

'I remember she screamed and screamed,' he said, 'and when Charles told her to stop being tiresome, she screamed all the more.'

'I wouldn't know. Having hit her, I went and spent the evening with my parents. In the servants' quarters, where I belonged.'

Toby didn't comment.

'Valerie's changed a lot,' he said after a few moments. 'I think you'd like her now.'

Laurie very much doubted that.

'She thinks I'm mad for allowing the general public anywhere near the Hall,' he went on. 'Perhaps she's right.'

'No,' Laurie said confidently. 'There's no

point in having somewhere as beautiful as Kingsley Hall, no point in designing the gardens and making them something special – no point to any of it if no-one sees it. You need to share it, to know what people feel about it, to hear their ideas.' She broke off. 'That's my view, for what it's worth.'

'I shall enjoy showing it off, but I'm not sure about the rest of it.' He brightened. 'But it's not as if it will be open to the public twenty-four hours a day, seven days a week.'

'Exactly.'

They stopped for lunch and to stretch their legs, then completed the rest of the journey without a break. It was five-thirty when they finally walked into their hotel.

As they were checking in, Laurie was already thinking about her mauve dress. Toby however, surprised her by suggesting a walk before dinner.

After spending so many hours in the car, Laurie thought it an excellent idea, and they arranged to meet in an hour.

Laurie had time to take a bath, unpack clothes which, she was pleased to see, weren't too creased, and relax. She'd never been to Inverness, and the capital of the Highlands was a delight.

'I didn't realise it ever got this warm so far north,' she said, as they headed for the river.

'I'm sure it's rare,' Toby agreed, smiling.

Laurie was wearing a lightweight jacket but most people, like Toby, were in shirt sleeves.

They stood on the bridge, gazing at the river beneath them. Toby's arm went around her shoulders in a gesture that seemed completely natural. It was tempting to move closer to him, to slip her arm around his waist...

Tempting, but madness.

'Laurie.' Toby's serious tone made her heartbeat quicken. 'What happened twenty years ago is history. It shouldn't make any difference to us.'

'Ah, but it does.'

He reached for her left hand, and turned it over in his own.

Surely he must be able to feel her racing, erratic pulse. As his gaze was fixed on her face, he would see her panic, too.

She was panicking because she thought he was about to kiss her. Panicking even more because she wanted him to...

When he did, his hands cupping her face, Laurie had to cling to his shoulders for support. His kiss was everything – infinitely tender, yet deeply passionate. Laurie was dizzy with longing.

It's only a kiss, she told herself helplessly, but she knew it wasn't only anything.

When he finally pulled back, his eyes dark and questioning, she felt suddenly bereft.

His hands still cupped her face, and her own refused to leave his shoulders.

As the water swirled beneath them, Laurie knew that nothing could be the same again...

CHAPTER TEN

Laurie was too dazed by Toby's kiss to think coherently until a single raindrop hit her face, bringing her back to reality.

'We'd better head back to the hotel before we get soaked,' She was unable even to look at Toby.

'Laurie–' He caught her hand to halt her flight, and she ended up far too close to him. He ran a gentle finger down her cheek. 'I love you,' he said simply.

'Please, don't!'

'I believe you have feelings for me, too,' he persisted.

'Please – let's get back to the hotel.'

With a sigh, he nodded.

'Come on, then.' His hand was still holding hers. 'Perhaps some food will help you face facts.'

Laurie was finding it difficult to breathe, never mind eat...

Sitting in his parents' conservatory, with a stunning view of the hills, Alan Watson had finally become real to Laurie, and her heart went out to the two people opposite her.

Until now, he'd simply been the curate – the man who'd vanished, the man she'd once believed responsible for the Kingsley Hall burglary, the man whose body had been found in the lake. Now, he was this lovely couple's son.

While Jessie Watson showed them photographs of her happy, smiling son, Angus made them another cup of tea.

'People around Kingsley thought he'd committed suicide,' Jessie said, 'but I never believed that. Alan wouldn't have done such a thing.'

'How did he like Kingsley?' Laurie asked. 'Was he happy there?'

'He was at first.' Jessie smiled suddenly. 'He'd imagined Lancashire as being full of grimy old mill towns, and the reality came as a pleasant surprise. He soon fell in love with the place, and he loved walking across the Pennines. According to him, Lancashire was almost as beautiful as it is here.'

Her smile faded.

'He liked the place and the people well enough,' she said, 'but I don't think he was happy in his work. It wasn't what he said so much as what he didn't say, but I don't think he liked the vicar.' She thought for a moment. In fact, I think he took a dislike to him. That wasn't like Alan at all. Perhaps I'm wrong. I know Reverend Casper did a lot of good work. And there was someone else – oh, what was his name? A lawyer. He and Alan were working together on fundraising for the church–'

'Daniel Armstrong?' Laurie asked.

'That's him!'

'I don't suppose you know what happened to him, do you?' Toby asked. 'We've been trying to track him down, but he seems to have vanished.'

'Oh, I wouldn't know.'

Angus came back with the tea tray, and Jessie rose to pour out.

'We kept the cuttings about what happened to your father,' Angus told Toby. 'A terrible business all round.'

'It was, and still is, something of a mystery.' Toby was about to say more, looked at Laurie and changed his mind.

So the Watsons didn't know who she was! Laurie took a deep breath.

'My father was butler at the hall at the time. He spent twelve years in prison.'

Jessie and Angus were too shocked to respond.

'He was innocent–' Laurie's voice trailed away.

'That's why we're keen to discover anything we can,' Toby explained for her. 'We think it's too coincidental that your son was murdered shortly before my father was.'

'So you think there's a connection?' Angus asked.

'We don't know,' Toby admitted, 'but we do know that Alan met my father. According to my housekeeper, he seemed quite agitated at the time.'

'Did Alan ever mention a lady called Ivy Bleasdon?' Laurie asked.

The Watsons looked at each other, then shook their heads.

'Means nothing to me,' Angus said, 'but it's all a long time ago. He might have mentioned her in passing. If he did, we've forgotten.'

That was a huge part of the problem. Too many years had blurred people's memories.

Toby turned the talk to Alan in happier times, and Laurie was pleased to see Jessie and Angus laughing at their memories.

She was so proud of Toby. He was caring, considerate and understanding – people were immediately at ease with him.

Laurie, though, was anything but at ease with him at the moment. Every time she glanced his way, her stomach turned a somersault and she was standing on that bridge again, reliving every moment of his kiss. She could still feel his mouth on hers–

And he had said he loved her!

In a perfect world, she should have been

the happiest girl alive. She'd have loved to throw herself into his arms, and tell him she would rather die than spend her life without him…

The thought had her heart breaking.

'His closest friend was Peter Graham,' Angus was saying. 'He's a priest in Inverness now.'

'Peter's lovely,' Jessie put in. 'Always sends a card on birthdays and at Christmas.'

Jessie left the conservatory and returned moments later with a letter, which she handed to Laurie.

'He sent this for my birthday last week.'

Laurie felt awkward reading a private letter. She only skimmed it quickly, but the man's warmth and humour leapt off the page. Peter Graham did indeed seem a lovely man.

Without intending to, Laurie had memorised his address, but she wouldn't go behind the Watsons' backs.

'Do you think he'd be willing to talk to us?' she asked.

'I'm sure he would.' Jessie hunted through an assortment of magazines and newspapers that were lying on the coffee table, found a pen and paper, and wrote down his address.

'You'll find him easily enough.'

Another hour passed before they left, during which time Jessie showed them yet more photographs, this time of Alan and Peter – two laughing teenagers.

'What now?' Toby asked as they were driving away from the Watsons' home. 'Shall we try to see Peter Graham?'

'We've nothing to lose.'

They probably had nothing to gain, either, Laurie thought grimly. It was unlikely Peter Graham would be able to tell them anything.

Despair had taken a firm grip now.

Twenty years ago, the police, with all their experience and technology, had investigated the curate's disappearance, the burglary at the Hall and the death of Toby's father. If there had been any evidence available, they would have found it.

What could Laurie hope to find twenty years later?

'The truth always comes out in the end,' Toby said, and she looked at him in amazement. Had he read her mind? It was difficult to tell, as he was concentrating on the road ahead.

'Don't despair, Laurie. The truth's there. It's simply a matter of finding it, and we won't give up until we have.'

Laurie nodded. She was absurdly close to tears. In whichever direction she looked life seemed one big tangled mess.

At six o'clock that evening, Laurie and Toby shook hands with Peter Graham. He'd been out when they first called and his housekeeper had suggested they come back.

'He usually gets an hour's peace between six and seven.'

The man himself came as a surprise to Laurie. That morning they'd been looking at photographs of him as a teenager, so she'd been expecting a man in his twenties. Ridiculous to forget that the last twenty years had left their mark on him, too.

Peter Graham was a short, balding man in his mid to late forties, with a firm handshake and a ready smile.

'Jessie warned me to expect you,' he said.

What an odd choice of word!

He ushered them into a large, cluttered sitting-room. Books, newspapers and pamphlets littered every surface.

'It's good to meet you both,' he added. 'Please, sit down.'

Laurie and Toby sat on the sofa, after Peter had scooped up several periodicals, looked around in vain for an empty space, and put them on the floor.

As soon as the social niceties were out of the way, Toby began explaining the reason behind their visit.

'We're convinced there's a connection between the murder of Alan Watson and my father. As I'm sure you can imagine, I want to know what really happened to my father and Laurie wants her father's name cleared.'

Peter Graham was thoughtful, and his thoughts seemed to trouble him, or perhaps that was Laurie's over-active imagination.

'It was a terrible shock to learn that Alan had been murdered,' he said at last. 'Even now, that hasn't quite sunk in. A terrible shock.'

Laurie and Toby remained seated as the priest paced the length of the room.

'When someone vanishes like that, you fear the worst,' he went on. 'You think of accidents. Alan was an outdoor person – I wondered if perhaps he'd gone swimming and found himself caught up in strong currents, or perhaps he'd gone hill walking and fallen–' He broke off and gave them a vague smile. 'Even so, you still expect that person to be alive. Hope is a very powerful ally.'

'It is,' Laurie agreed quietly. 'Did Alan speak to you of his life in Kingsley?'

There was a brief hesitation.

'He did, yes. I teased him relentlessly, thinking he wouldn't settle south of the border. He'd trained in the south, but that's different.' He smiled that vague, sad smile again. 'He loved the place. And the people, too.'

'He was happy in his work?' Laurie asked.

Again that hesitation.

'I imagine so.'

'How did he get on with the vicar?' Toby asked. 'Did he say?'

'He respected him, but I'm not sure he took

to the man. They got along well enough, though.'

'He was also working with a lawyer, a man called Daniel Armstrong,' Toby pressed on. 'Do you know if they got along well?'

'Why do you ask?'

It wasn't Laurie's imagination; Peter Graham's responses were guarded.

'My father kept a journal,' Toby explained. 'It seems he considered Armstrong a dangerous man.'

'Dangerous? That's a strong word. May I ask if your father recorded details of that meeting?'

'My father was killed that night,' Toby told him, and Laurie watched as every vestige of colour left Peter Graham's face.

Then his telephone rang.

Laurie hoped the housekeeper would answer, but Peter answered it himself.

Her heart sank on listening to his side of the conversation.

'I'm sorry to hear that ... yes, thank you... I'll be there as soon as I can.'

He replaced the receiver.

'I'm sorry, but I need to get to the hospital. A parishioner.' He took a deep breath.

'I also need to think over all you've said, and you must remember that some things Alan told me were confidential. However, knowing Alan was murdered has put a whole new light on things. Look, I'm sorry, but I must go. My housekeeper will show you out.'

'Do you remember if Alan mentioned a woman called Ivy Bleasdon?' Toby put in quickly as they rose to their feet.

Peter Graham froze.

'Yes,' he replied. 'I do remember.'

His expression was grim.

'I must think it over. Leave your phone number with my housekeeper and I'll be in touch. Now, I'm sorry, but I must dash.'

They gave his housekeeper every contact number they had, and left, hoping.

'He knows something, doesn't he?' Laurie said, as soon as they were sitting in Toby's car.

'I think he probably does.'

'Do you think he'll get in touch?'

'I do,' Toby said carefully, 'but whether he'll be able to tell us much is a different matter. If Alan Watson mentioned something in confidence—'

'Yes, but as he said, the man was murdered. Surely that changes everything.'

'We'll see. I suggest we give him a week, then jog his memory. Meanwhile,' he added, smiling a heart-stopping smile, 'let's eat...'

Three days later, Laurie was sitting in Toby's car again, her hands clenching and unclenching. She was angry because he'd phoned her dad last night without her knowledge.

Perhaps she had every right to be angry.

218

Toby knew, however, that he and her father needed to talk.

She was nervous, Toby suspected, because she didn't think it would be an easy meeting. Yet, although he and her father had only spoken briefly, it had seemed to Toby that Jim Whitney was keen for them to meet.

'I know your father hasn't been well, Laurie,' he said, 'and I promise I won't say anything to upset him. I'm not without feeling, you know.'

Her head flew up.

'I know you're not, but – well, you've spent the biggest part of your life hating Dad. It's going to be difficult.'

'I did hate him,' Toby agreed frankly, 'but only because I believed he'd killed my father for the sake of a few jewels.'

'For all you know, that's exactly what he did,' she retorted.

Yes, Laurie was angry.

'I know he's innocent now. Don't ask me how I know – it's nothing to do with wishful thinking, nothing to do with my feelings for you, nothing–'

'Toby, don't!' She cut him off.

'I just know he's innocent. I know it in the same way I know the earth's round.'

In the same way I know that I love you, he added silently.

She said nothing, and returned her gaze to the scenery. Toby doubted she took note of anything they passed.

He wasn't as calm about this meeting with Jim Whitney as he appeared. It was going to be far from easy. But with so many new questions coming to light, it was just possible Jim might remember something...

Toby couldn't dismiss the look on Peter Graham's face when he'd heard Ivy Bleasdon's name. For the man to remember one name, after twenty years, was unbelievable.

Toby's own father had been concerned about her, and the young curate had mentioned her to his best friend.

Ivy Bleasdon, eighty-three, had died suddenly – but there, many eighty-three-year-olds did. If, as Toby's imagination insisted on suggesting, she was murdered... No, it was absurd. The doctors would have found something.

For all that, he'd talked to Terri Marshall, and Terri had promised to find out all she could about Ivy Bleasdon's sudden death...

Toby's mind was still going round in circles when, having followed Laurie's brisk directions, he stopped the car outside a small block of flats.

It looked a pleasant enough area, where residents took pride in their homes, gardens and cars. Toby was only allowed that fleeting impression because Jim Whitney was at his door.

Toby wouldn't have recognised him. It was

Jim Whitney, however, because Laurie had raced up the path to fling her arms around him.

Toby couldn't remember ever being so nervous about meeting anyone.

Jim Whitney didn't appear to have such problems. There was a huge smile on his face and his hand was outstretched long before Toby reached it. His own hand was grasped firmly.

'Well, well, well!' Jim said, chuckling. 'Funny how the mind plays tricks some-times, isn't it? I was half-expecting a gangly thirteen-year-old lad in his school uniform. Ah, but it's so good to see you again. May I call you Toby?'

'So long as I'm allowed to call you Jim.'

'It's a deal.'

They went inside. Thanks to Laurie firing questions at her father, Toby was saved from further conversation – just as well, because Jim's warm welcome had brought a huge lump to his throat.

'Steve's in the area,' Jim was saying to Laurie. 'Did you know? He's making one of his flying visits.' He chuckled. 'When are his visits anything else?'

'I didn't know.' Laurie didn't look pleased by the news.

Toby was still wondering who Steve was when he realised that they were discussing Laurie's ex-husband.

'He said he'd try to call in before he heads back to Scotland,' Jim went on, 'so I thought he might have been here by now. Still, there's plenty of time. Perhaps we'll all have lunch together.'

Jim looked delighted by this prospect, but Toby was horrified. The last thing he needed was to come face to face with the man Laurie had once been in love with! And perhaps still was in love with, for all Toby knew.

'That'll be good,' Laurie said, and Toby couldn't decide if the prospect pleased her or not.

While he was trying to fathom that out, the man himself arrived.

Toby's first impression as he watched Steve Summerfield take Laurie in his arms and swing her off her feet, was of a big, handsome, strong-looking man.

'I've heard a lot about you.' Steve shook Toby's hand warmly. 'It's good to meet you at last. Laurie's showed me plans of the gardens at Kingsley Hall, and I can't wait to see it. You must be very excited about it.'

'Yes,' Toby agreed, hoping that covered everything. Then, deciding it didn't, he asked Steve about his own work.

He was, Toby had to admit, a very know-ledgeable man who cared deeply about con-servation.

'But don't get me going on that,' Steve said, grinning, 'or we'll be here all day. I thought I'd buy you lunch, then shoot off.'

Both Jim and Laurie thought this a wonderful idea, and Toby felt obliged to pretend likewise.

They decided to drive out to a pub near the river, with two cars, so that Steve could drive straight to Scotland. This suited Toby – until he watched Laurie drive off with Steve.

'They seem to get along very well,' Toby remarked, as he concentrated on the car in front rather than its passengers.

'Heartening, isn't it?' Jim replied happily, not realising that Toby was far from heartened. 'They'll always be the best of friends. Seems odd that they couldn't make a go of their marriage. No spark, you see.'

'Ah.'

'So, young Toby, what's the Hall looking like these days? Is it still the same?'

'Apart from a team of groundsmen, and diggers and bulldozers everywhere – yes, it's still the same.'

Jim smiled at that.

'A truly beautiful place,' he said. 'I hope this new venture of yours is a success. The cost of keeping a place like that going must be frightening.'

'It is, but thanks to Laurie, I think people will be keen to see the grounds.'

'I'm sure they will. My Anne always swore it was the most beautiful place on earth.'

Toby wasn't sure how to respond to that. Perhaps what surprised him most was that Jim Whitney showed no sign of bitterness. He'd lost twelve years of his life, and a great deal more, yet there was no bitterness.

'We will get your name cleared, Jim,' he said, his voice thick. 'I'm sure of it.'

Jim looked taken aback for a moment, but recovered quickly.

'Maybe, maybe not. But know this, Toby, I would never have harmed a hair on your father's head. He gave me everything, and I'll always be indebted to him. If someone had to die that night, I'd rather it had been me. At least that way I'd have known my Anne and young Laurie would have been taken care of. As it was – well.' He left the rest unsaid. 'It's only another mile or so down here.'

Toby was surprised to find lunch wasn't too much of an ordeal. Laurie and Steve were very good friends, and Toby was jealous of the history they shared, but he could see that Laurie didn't look at Steve in the same way she looked at him.

Jim had said there was no spark between them, and Toby understood exactly what he meant. When Laurie looked at Toby, that spark was there...

Sitting outside where the tables overlooked the river, they talked of Laurie's work at the Hall, and Steve's work in Scotland. Inevitably, they then discussed Toby and Laurie's trip north.

'What do you remember of Alan Watson?' Steve asked Jim.

'Not a lot, I'm afraid. He seemed a pleasant enough young chap, but I didn't have a lot to do with him. We'd pass the time of day, discuss the weather, that sort of thing, but nothing more.'

'And what about the vicar?' Toby asked. 'What was he like? Some people seem to have disliked the man.'

'I think he was one of those types you either loved or hated,' Jim said. 'Many folk liked him.' He shrugged. 'And many didn't. He could be abrupt, a bit aloof, but I'm sure he was a good man at heart. He certainly did a lot for the community, and was involved with several charities.'

'So we've heard,' Toby murmured. 'And what about Daniel Armstrong?'

'Now there was a man I couldn't take to at all,' Jim said. 'Your father didn't like him, either. Not that he said as much to me,' he added quickly, 'but it was clear enough to see. Although why he considered him a dangerous man, I don't know. That's a puzzle. At first, Armstrong was a regular visitor at the Hall, but that tailed off. He was a social climber. Wanted power and money. When he knew someone had money, he'd be there – making out he was their best friend.'

'The curate was working closely with him on some fundraising project,' Toby said. 'Do you know anything about that?'

Jim shook his head.

'Well, Armstrong vanished into thin air – about six months after Alan Watson went missing and my father was killed.'

Jim stared at Toby.

'Have they come up with anything new on that chap who claimed he was a fine arts dealer?' Steve asked curiously. 'What was his name? Charles Taylor?'

'That's him.' Jim nodded. 'Real name Victor Smith. He admits to calling at the Hall when I said he did, and he admits to wanting to eye up the place, but at the time of the burglary, he was in police custody. A nice alibi, that.'

'Could he have had anything to do with the murder of the curate?' Steve asked, frowning. 'Was he in police custody then?'

'They questioned him. He's in the clear,' Laurie said. 'At the moment, the police are getting nowhere fast.'

'It all happened such a long time ago,' Jim reminded them.

'That's true,' Steve agreed. 'Laurie and I were – what? Eight at the time?

'What about you, Toby?'

'I was thirteen, and Jim's right, that's the problem. Memories have dulled, evidence has been lost.'

They fell silent, acknowledging the truth of that.

'Coffee?' Steve suggested.

Toby accepted, but had he known that Jim and Laurie would decide on a walk down to the river instead, he would have refused, too. As it was, he was left alone with Steve.

'I would love to know what really happened that night,' Steve murmured, watching father and daughter. 'Jim deserves to learn the truth. Laurie, too.'

'Yes, they do,' Toby agreed.

'So do you,' Steve put in hastily. 'I suppose we're all so wrapped up in the injustice Jim suffered that we tend to forget you lost your father that night.'

'That's understandable,' Toby acknowledged.

Steve watched Laurie and Jim for a few moments.

'Laurie's very happy at Kingsley, isn't she?' he murmured.

Toby wasn't quite sure what to make of that.

'I believe so, yes,' he said. 'She loves her work, and she loves the Hall.'

'What about you?' Steve said quietly. 'Does she love you?'

Toby was taken aback. You had to admire the man's frankness, though, and he knew that Steve was only interested in Laurie's welfare.

'I hope so,' he answered.

Steve gazed at him, then nodded slowly.

'Yes, so do I. I also hope this new venture of yours is a huge success. Laurie's appetite could bankrupt a man.'

They were still laughing at that when Jim and Laurie returned.

'What's so funny?' Laurie asked.

'You are,' Steve said, getting to his feet. 'And now I'm off. If I don't make a start, I'll hit the motorways at the wrong time...'

He said his goodbyes and shook Toby's hand.

'Good to meet you, Toby,' he said.

'You, too. I hope we meet again soon.'

'Good luck,' Steve added. 'With everything...'

Laurie was thoughtful as Toby drove them back to Kingsley Hall. It had been a strange couple of days in Middlesex.

Dad looked fit and well, and it had been wonderful to see him. Good to see him and Toby together, too.

She hadn't imagined the two of them getting on so well, and the respect between them had taken her completely by surprise.

After her initial doubts, it had been good to see Steve, too. At first, she'd been afraid with him and Toby together. She'd be bound to compare them.

She hadn't, though. It was impossible. They couldn't be more different.

She loved Steve as a friend, and knew he felt the same. Toby she loved in a completely different way. She didn't want to love him, had tried everything she knew not to love him, but love him she did.

She loved him in a way that meant she didn't feel quite whole when she wasn't with him...

'What were you and Steve laughing about?' she asked him. 'At lunch, when Dad and I came back from the river?'

'You.'

Which told her nothing.

'And?'

Toby gave her a sideways glance, checked his rear-view mirror, and then indicated to pull off the motorway.

He drove for a few hundred yards, then parked in a quiet lay-by edged with tall trees.

Switching off the engine, he turned to face her.

'Steve was wishing me luck with everything at the Hall,' he said slowly. 'He thought I'd need the income. Seemed to think your appetite could bankrupt a man.'

Laurie didn't laugh.

'What? Did he – I mean, does he imagine that you and I–?' She couldn't put her questions into words.

'He seems to believe we have a future, yes,' Toby said. 'All I need to do now is convince you, Laurie.'

At the moment, Laurie thought that wouldn't take much doing.

She felt different today. Had the stumbling block been Dad? Yet her father liked and respected Toby, and her ex-husband seemed to feel the same way.

In any case, it wasn't their life. It was hers! She could either allow herself to love Toby or...

Or what? She couldn't imagine her future without him.

'Perhaps I'm already convinced.'

He reached for her hands, and held them in his.

'I love you,' she told him, and the surprise on his face matched her own. She had believed she would never be able to tell him so.

She suddenly wanted to shout it out to the world, but she couldn't. She was too busy being kissed...

'You'll marry me?' Toby asked, his lips still close to her own.

She hadn't thought that far ahead. Yet she loved him, she knew she would go to her grave loving him.

'Yes. Yes, I'll marry you, Toby...'

When Toby finally turned the car into the drive at Kingsley Hall, the first thing they saw was Terri's car parked outside Laurie's cottage, and Terri herself hammering on

Laurie's door.

Laurie's first thought on seeing the private investigator who had soon become her friend was to leap out of the car and tell her the news. But the silly grin she'd been wearing for the past hours slipped.

'What now?' she said anxiously.

'We'll soon find out.' Toby gave her hand a reassuring squeeze.

Terri dashed over to them, her ever-present bulging shoulder-bag swinging against jeans-clad legs.

'This lawyer of ours,' she said breathlessly. 'It seems he took off for Spain less than six months after your dad was charged, Laurie.'

'Spain? Why Spain?' Laurie got out of the car.

'I don't know,' Terri admitted, 'and I don't know what he's been doing for the last twenty years. However, I passed that on to the police, and they're obviously taking it seriously. Very seriously indeed. They're already in touch with the Spanish police.'

'Really?' Toby put an arm around Laurie's shoulders. 'Come on – let's go up to the house and see what we can find out. I think a few phone calls are in order...'

When the three of them reached the Hall, Sally was there to greet them, more concerned about feeding them than anything else.

'By the way, Toby, a man's been trying to

speak to you. I gave him your mobile number, but he said he wouldn't bother you until you were back. A Scottish chap. A priest.'

'Peter Graham!'

Toby rang the number at once, but there was no reply.

'We'll ring our favourite detective,' Toby decided.

It took a while to get through to Superintendent Phillips, and even then, Laurie only heard Toby's side of the conversation.

'So Mr Graham called you yesterday?' he said, frowning. 'I see … and you've no idea where Daniel Armstrong is? Yes, yes, I quite understand…'

When Toby replaced the receiver, Laurie couldn't read his face.

'It seems,' he said at last, 'that Daniel Armstrong may have conned Ivy Bleasdon, Kathleen Eve, and a number of other vulnerable, elderly women out of a small fortune. Following the phone call he had from Peter Graham, Detective Phillips believes that Alan Watson found out about this and confided his worries to my father – and to Peter.'

Toby grasped Laurie's shoulders, as if to help his words sink in.

'Laurie, Armstrong may have killed Alan Watson and my father because they knew too much…'

CHAPTER ELEVEN

'So when's the big day?' Dave asked, and Laurie had to laugh. It was a question everyone wanted answering.

'If it were up to Toby,' she told him as they walked towards the almost completed rose garden, 'it would be tomorrow. As I have some say in the matter, it'll be after Christmas – weeks before we open to the public.'

A week had passed since she'd accepted Toby's proposal, and she still couldn't quite believe it. For the rest of her days, she would live with Toby as his wife. She would be Mrs Davis, and they would live at the Hall, watch their children explore every inch of the grounds, just as they had themselves, grow old together...

'We'll get an invite, I hope?' Toby's foreman said.

'You certainly will!' She laughed at the absurdity of the question. 'The whole of Kingsley will be there. I want a huge wedding!'

Dave pulled a face.

'Not a black tie do, I hope?' He shuddered.

'Now there's a thought,' she said, grinning at him.

'A thought best forgotten,' he told her sternly. 'The last time I went to one of those–'

He broke off as a police car came along the drive.

'I wonder what they want?'

'I don't know, but I intend to find out. Excuse me, Dave...'

Rubbing grubby hands on her jeans, Laurie headed for the Hall. If there was any news at all, she wanted to hear it.

Over the past week, the media had grown more and more interested in Daniel Armstrong. It seemed as if Detective Superintendent Phillips was never off the television screen. Even the national coverage was increasing on a daily basis.

For all that, Armstrong still hadn't been traced.

Fortunately, Laurie had had a busy week, but her mind refused to budge from the investigation. Was it possible, after all these years, that her dad's name was about to be cleared?

Every morning, she awoke confident in the knowledge that the truth would soon come to light. Every night, she despaired of more evidence being found...

Toby was standing on the steps to the Hall when the superintendent climbed out of his car.

They went into the library.

'I thought I'd update you, and it's not good news, I'm afraid, Daniel Armstrong died twelve years ago.'

'No!'

Laurie didn't know whether to scream and shout at the injustice of that, or fall to the floor and weep. She didn't have the strength for either.

If Daniel Armstrong had been guilty – and she knew he was – they would never be able to prove it. He would have taken his secrets to the grave.

'We're trying to trace a Spanish lawyer he had dealings with,' Phillips explained. 'Meanwhile, we're investigating his financial affairs. That's a nightmare in itself – bank accounts have been closed and records destroyed. Believe me, needles in haystacks would be easy compared to this.'

And what was the point?

'At least we've got something to pin on him, thanks to your friend Peter Graham.'

'I spoke to Peter this morning,' Toby put in. 'He's feeling quite bad about it all. Apparently, he'd warned Alan to be careful. It seems my father wasn't the only one to consider Armstrong dangerous. It was on Peter's suggestion that the curate confided in my father.'

'It seems as if Alan Watson paid with his life for knowing too much about Armstrong's affairs.'

'And Toby's dad did the same?' Laurie asked.

'We've no evidence to support that,' the detective answered her, 'but yes, that's what I believe.'

'So now you believe my father's innocent?' She stood tall as she faced him, and he looked at her long and hard.

'What I believe doesn't count for much, I'm afraid. As I said, we have no evidence.' His tone softened as he saw her frustration. 'All the evidence is circumstantial, and it happened twenty years ago.'

His phone rang then, and he wandered over to the window.

'That's very interesting.' His thoughtful gaze was fixed on Laurie, so she knew he was discussing her dad's case.

When he ended the call, he looked at them both for a long time before he spoke.

'We've come across details of another bank account held by Armstrong. There was never much in it, and it was dormant much of the time, but the day before Mr Davis was killed, the sum of two thousand pounds was withdrawn. In cash.'

Laurie gasped.

'The money that was sent to my father!'

'We don't know that,' he said patiently.

'Oh, tosh! Of course we do,' Laurie cried. 'That man framed him! The bundle of cash delivered to my father was the only real piece of evidence you had. Because of that, Dad spent twelve years of his life behind bars.' She felt the sting of tears in her eyes and had to blink rapidly.

'But dead men don't talk, do they?'

The superintendent gave her shoulder a reassuring squeeze.

'Live men don't always talk, either,' he said drily. 'We want evidence, not talk.'

'There is no evidence, though,' Laurie burst out. 'My dad spent twelve years in a cell, and his life was ruined. Toby lost his father. Alan Watson's life was cut tragically short. Ivy Bleasdon, Kathleen Eve and countless others were swindled – and there's nothing we can do about it!'

'I'm leaving for Spain shortly,' the detective told them. 'I'll be in touch.'

As they stood watching him drive off, Toby slipped his arm around Laurie's waist.

'We're getting there, love,' he said confidently.

'Are we?' Laurie wasn't so sure. 'You know and I know that Armstrong's guilty but with no evidence–'

'There will be evidence,' Toby said. 'Twenty years ago, Armstrong wasn't suspected of a thing, so he wasn't even questioned.'

'Now he's dead, so he still can't be questioned,' Laurie put in.

'I've great faith in Phillips. He'll find that evidence.'

'You think so?'

'Yes, I do.' He wrapped his arms around her. 'Meanwhile, we have a wedding to plan.'

Whenever Toby kissed her, all her troubles vanished and the world was a just, fair place. Oh, how she loved this man!

'We have a honeymoon to plan, too,' he added. 'Where shall we go?'

'I get a honeymoon as well?' She laughed.

'Of course. You'll need it before you begin a life of poverty with me.'

'A life of poverty? Ha! People will flock to see my gardens.'

They linked arms and walked into the rose garden.

'A honeymoon,' she mused. 'Italy would be nice.'

'Whereabouts?'

'Anywhere,' she said dreamily. 'Let's tour Italy. See where the mood takes us...'

On Sunday, Laurie and Toby met up with detective Terri Marshall and her husband, Adam, for lunch.

Needless to say, there was just one topic of conversation – Daniel Armstrong.

'I heard on the grapevine late yesterday that Armstrong's cleaner at the time had volunteered some useful information.'

'Oh? Such as?' Laurie gazed at Terri's policeman husband.

'I don't know,' he admitted.

'She was in her late teens when she worked for him,' Terri reported, 'and left around the time the curate went missing.'

That sounded interesting. Laurie would love to be the proverbial fly on the wall at that police station.

'Is there any news on the cash Armstrong withdrew from his bank account?' she asked. 'My dad was convicted on the strength of that.'

'Nothing,' Adam told her.

'He's definitely guilty,' Laurie said, frowning.

'Without doubt,' Adam agreed. 'The problem is proving it.'

'How's your dad holding up, Laurie?' Terri asked.

'Amazingly well. He doesn't seem too concerned about Armstrong being *proved* guilty. As far as Dad's concerned, Armstrong's the culprit, and that's enough.'

'But what about all those years he spent locked up? There could be compensation...'

'He believes you can't change the past. You can only look forward to the future. As he said, Armstrong's dead, whereas he's still here.'

Terri smiled at that.

'Talking of the future, I bet he's looking forward to walking you up the aisle.'

'He's like a kid at Christmas,' Laurie said

on a splutter of laughter.

To say her father had been thrilled by the news of his only daughter's forthcoming marriage was putting it mildly.

'It's funny,' he'd said, 'but when you and Toby were kids, your mum always reckoned you were made for each other. She'd be so pleased, love...'

Much as Laurie wished Mum could share in the celebrations, she knew he was right, and that helped enormously.

She wouldn't think of Mum's absence, though. Instead, she would remember the close, loving relationship she'd shared with her, and think of how happy Mum would be to see father and daughter walking up the aisle towards Toby.

After a pleasant lunch that had stretched across most of the afternoon, Toby was in need of exercise and fresh air.

'Why don't we reward Holly's patience by taking her for a walk across the moor?' he suggested.

'In these shoes?' Laurie looked down at her feet. 'Oh come on, then. At least I'm not wearing heels, and it should be dry.'

A strong wind was blowing, and keeping to the track for the sake of Laurie's shoes meant that it was hard work. They were soon breathless

For all that, the view was stunning. The

hills stretched for miles.

'The view is constantly changing, isn't it?' Laurie mused. 'Look at the way the sun is lighting up that old barn. And the church.'

'Not to mention the Hall.' He pointed. 'It looks very grand. See how the main path stretches down to the lake – perfectly straight!'

She punched him playfully on the arm.

'Of course it's straight. It took us ages to sort that out.' She grinned at him. 'Perhaps when all the visitors are tramping around we'll come up here and watch them.'

'Sounds perfect to me.'

Laurie sat on the old stone wall and gazed at the Hall and grounds, a look of complete satisfaction on her face.

'Isn't it strange how life has a habit of coming full circle?' she remarked. 'As a child, I loved every inch of the Hall, the grounds and the surrounding hills. Then, when we were banished, I believed I'd never see any of it again.'

That 'banished' hurt. The injustice of it all hurt, and Toby often wondered what his father would have said if he'd known Jim Whitney had lost so much for a crime he hadn't committed.

'If I'd had my way and gone to university,' Laurie went on, 'I would never have gone to horticultural college, never have studied under Des, never had my name put forward for this job.'

'But you did.'

As Toby sat on the wall beside her, he thought how empty his life would be without her. It was lucky for him that life did have a habit of coming full circle.

'I wonder what Armstrong's cleaner told the police?' he murmured.

'I don't know, but if it were of great interest, surely she would have told them twenty years ago.'

'But twenty years ago, she didn't know Armstrong was robbing people of their life savings. Nor did she know that the curate had been murdered.'

'True.'

'Something that might have seemed perfectly innocent at the time could have taken on a whole new meaning.'

'I suppose so. Isn't it a long, slow process, though? Nothing new comes to light.'

'The police need to check and re-check every fact,' Toby pointed out. 'As Phillips said, they need hard evidence.'

'A pity they weren't so enthusiastic for hard evidence twenty years ago,' Laurie muttered grimly.

They talked of other things – their wedding plans, Italy, childhood memories – and Laurie's frown was soon replaced by the smile Toby loved so much.

The walk back to the car was made even

slower by Holly who found a huge stick and insisted they throw it for her.

'Was there ever a more pointless game?' Toby said, stroking the dog's ears as she waited for him to hurl the stick as far as he could.

Eventually, they persuaded her to leave her stick behind and climb into the back of the car so they could drive home.

Sally was on the front steps waiting for them, looking as if she'd been there for hours. As soon as she saw the car, she began waving her arms frantically.

'What now?' Laurie asked anxiously.

Toby only hoped it wasn't bad news. His first thought was that Laurie's father had suffered another heart attack.

Please, no, he prayed. Not before the wedding, not when we're so close to discovering the truth!

Sally raced down the steps and began talking before they were even out of the car.

'The phone hasn't stopped ... that policeman, and that investigator girl, Terri Marshall–' Sally suddenly burst into tears.

'It was Daniel Armstrong who murdered your father, Toby!'

'So tell me again,' Micky insisted, 'exactly what happened.'

Jim was still shocked. He'd spent years praying for this day yet, deep down, he had never believed it would come.

All morning, he'd walked in the park, trying to get his thoughts in order, yet he was still shocked.

Back at his flat, trying to make tea for himself and Micky, his hands refused to stop shaking.

'Thanks to that priest Laurie and Toby visited in Scotland, the police knew that Armstrong had been lining his pockets by swindling the likes of Ivy Bleasdon and Kathleen Eve,' Jim explained, his voice still shaky. 'The young curate had his suspicions about Ivy, and confided in his best friend. Apparently, Armstrong had threatened young Alan. Anyway,' he continued, 'while the police were delving into his financial affairs, they discovered an entry showing two thousand pounds in cash had been withdrawn the day before Mr Edward was killed.'

'And been delivered to you?' Micky pulled a face. 'My, what I wouldn't like to do to that man.'

'Too late now,' Jim said quietly. 'It seems he knew he had cancer when he took off for Spain.'

'But why you, Jim? Why did he pick on you?'

'Because he knew the police would fall for it, I suppose,' Jim replied. 'Mr Edward had confronted him with what he knew, so Armstrong decided he had to get rid of him

– just as he'd got rid of Alan Watson. I was the easy target. I had access to the safe, so it was easy enough for me to carry out the burglary. Easy, too, to kill Mr Edward when he supposedly disturbed me.'

Micky had a few choice words to say on the matter.

'And then his cleaner went to the police,' Jim continued when Micky had stopped swearing. 'She'd had a row with him. Armstrong had been in a blind rage because she'd said something about his lifestyle. By all accounts, he lived like a king. At the time, she was seeing a young lad from the village. Her parents were against the relationship and so they used to sneak off and meet without anyone knowing. Armstrong must have done a bit of spying of his own because he found out about it and threatened her – said he'd tell her parents about it.'

'And?' Micky asked, frowning.

'Connie, that's the lass's name, and her young man decided to run away,' Jim said.

'Elope?'

'Something like that,' Jim said, smiling. 'They ran off to Brighton together. Still together now – happily married with five children. Anyway, the night they ran off was the night Mr Edward was killed. Connie and her young man had met in the village that night and were planning to walk to the bus stop, catch the bus into Manchester, and then the train to wherever it would take them.'

Jim found the story strangely romantic. Funny to think of the two young lovers running away while he'd been standing outside the Hall that night have a quiet smoke.

'They were walking towards the Hall when a car's headlights frightened them. They leapt into the hedge so as not to be seen, and then saw the headlights pick out Armstrong just ahead of them. He was carrying a can – petrol, I imagine, ready to burn the Hall to the ground.'

He smiled at that.

'I can picture the two of them, can't you, Micky? Holding their breath in the dark hedge?'

'Yes, but get to the point.' Micky had never been blessed with patience.

'According to Connie, when they eventually plucked up courage to peer out of their hedge, he was nowhere to be seen. Then they heard his footsteps, and saw a shadow walking up to the Hall.'

Micky shook his head in bewilderment.

'And they never had the sense to tell the police?'

'It wasn't that simple. The two of them lay low for a month or so, until they could be married. Only when the deed was done and it was too late to be dragged home did they contact their parents.'

'Yes, but–'

'By then,' Jim said, 'the burglary at the Hall, the death of Mr Edward and my being sent down for it all, were only mentioned in passing. It's only now, with the national papers picking up on Armstrong and reminding the world I've always protested my innocence, that Connie realised what Armstrong must have been up to.'

Jim took a long drink of tea.

'It didn't matter, though. At about the same time Connie was telling her story to the police, Superintendent Phillips was in Spain, talking to Armstrong's lawyer out there.'

Jim still couldn't quite believe it. To think that Armstrong's written confession had been lying around in a Spanish safe for all these years!

'But why,' Micky demanded in exasperation, 'didn't that Spanish lawyer pass on that confession?'

'It was in a sealed envelope, Armstrong had no family–' Jim shrugged.

At long last, the puzzle that had occupied them both for so long had been solved.

Jim's phone rang, but he ignored it.

'It'll be more reporters,' he told Micky. 'If it's anyone important, they'll leave a message and I'll call them back.'

Micky munched his way through a biscuit.

'It'll be the official pardon for you then, Jim,' he said, a grin breaking out. 'There ought to be a bit of compensation in it, too.'

Jim pulled a face.

'I don't care for any of that,' he said. 'All I ever wanted was for Laurie to know the truth. And Toby, too, of course.'

He felt the tension slowly begin to leave his body.

'It's over now – time to look to the future. And what a future it promises to be! I reckon I'll soon have grandchildren. Imagine that, Micky.'

'Give the lass a chance,' Micky spluttered. 'She's not even wed yet...'

Gazing up at the huge Sorrento moon, Laurie wondered if her dad was looking up at the same moon back in England.

What a wonderful man he was! Her heart filled with pride. His beaming smile had never left his face on her wedding day, and the speech he'd given at the reception had brought tears to her eyes.

Toby's speech had had a similar effect on her. His love had been there for all the world to see.

She gazed across the table at her husband as they sat outside a bar in Sorrento, prolonging a perfect evening. Laurie had a coffee in front of her; Toby coffee and a brandy. Toby, too, was gazing up at the huge moon.

Aware of her watching him, he smiled.

'Happy, Mrs Davis?'

'Happier than I ever thought possible.'

He reached for her hand.

'Then that makes two of us.'

'I was thinking about our wedding, and wondering if Dad stopped smiling all day.'

'Not that I noticed.' Toby laughed.

'It was a perfect day, wasn't it?'

'It was, my love.' He grinned suddenly. 'But so it should have been, given the length of time it took to organise.'

Laurie laughed. It had taken a lot of planning – yet there had been so much else going on.

It had taken time to accept what Armstrong had done. His crimes had clearly haunted him, right up until the end. It was still hard to believe that his confession, so full of remorse, had been sitting in a Spanish lawyer's office all these years.

As Toby had said, there was one reason to be grateful to Daniel Armstrong. He'd planned to burn Kingsley Hall to the ground, destroying any evidence Mr Edward might have gathered, yet his conscience had got the better of him and he'd called the fire brigade. If he hadn't, the Hall could well have been destroyed...

Christmas had soon been upon them. With only four months to go until Kingsley Hall was opened to the public for the first time, life had been hectic. Thankfully, work had gone without too many hitches, leaving Laurie and Toby free to plan their wedding.

And what a wedding it had been!

Kingsley's small church had been over-flowing with guests. When she and Toby had stepped out into the late February sunshine, the cameras hadn't stopped clicking.

And here they were in Sorrento, on the last day of their honeymoon. Tomorrow, they would catch the plane back to England.

Laurie had enjoyed every second of it – driving through the picturesque Tuscan countryside towards Pisa, past the beautiful riverside to the Leaning Tower; taking the steamer to Capri and visiting the Blue Grotto; seeing St Peter's Basilica; taking a gondola on Venice's Grand Canal – yet she wouldn't be sorry to leave Italy behind.

They'd been away for four weeks, and she longed to see the Hall again. It was home. God willing, it would be home for the rest of her days.

The plane was delayed by a couple of hours, but finally they touched down in Manchester. What a shock it was to step on to the tarmac and shiver! The sun was shining on this April morning, but it was having little effect on the temperature.

Laurie was pleased to climb inside the car and switch on the heater.

As they set off, she gazed with satisfaction at the passing countryside.

Beautiful though Italy was, England on a

sunny morning took some beating. Everywhere looked fresh and green, washed by
recent rain. Fields and hedgerows were
bursting with the promise of new life.

'I hope Dave's coped all right,' she said.
The last thing they needed was a last-min-
ute disaster before they opened the gates to
the public.

'I'm sure he has,' Toby took his eyes off the
road briefly to smile at her. 'I hope Sally's
been busy baking. I'm ready for some of her
home cooking.'

So was Laurie. Breakfast on the plane had
been very pleasant, but she was still hungry.

'And I hope our new butler is as good as
he's supposed to be,' Toby added.

'New butler?' Laurie stared at him in
disbelief. 'What do you mean – new butler?'

'I told you about him, didn't I?'

'No, you didn't! Oh, for heaven's sake,
Toby, what do we want with a butler? I
mean, who has a butler in this day and age?'

'I thought he'd be useful,' he said lamely,
'and when people visit – well, it looks better,
doesn't it? Besides, if we're busy with the
Hall and the grounds, and Sally's busy
feeding us and chasing around – well, I
thought it was a good idea.'

'It's a ridiculous idea!' Laurie retorted.
'We're not royalty, you know. Besides, I hate
the thought of strangers being in the Hall.'

A glint of light caught the ring Toby had

placed on her finger four weeks ago – the ring she would always treasure – and she sighed.

Why was she so peeved? Because she hated the thought of a stranger intruding in their lives? Because Toby had made a decision without consulting her? Or because she imagined a pretentious butler opening the Hall door would be off-putting to her friends?

Anyway, she knew she was being petty.

'Toby, will you stop the car for a moment, please?'

As soon as he'd switched off the engine, she linked her arm through his and rested her head against his shoulder.

'Sorry,' she murmured. 'I didn't mean to get angry.'

'That's you angry?' Amusement danced in his eyes. 'I've seen you a lot angrier than that.'

That was one of the things she loved most about him, the way he managed to make her laugh.

'Perhaps it was the thought of sharing you,' she said quietly. 'I've still got that honeymoon feeling, and I've enjoyed having you all to myself.' She looked into his face. 'I love you so very much, Toby.'

'I know you do, just as I love you.' He touched her chin lightly. 'And you won't be sharing me with anyone. Ever.'

She couldn't imagine why she'd been so

silly. Kingsley Hall was vast, and Toby was probably right in saying they needed more staff.

As they neared the Hall, Laurie was almost speechless with excitement. She couldn't wait to see the place.

Sally would be waiting to hear all about Italy, Holly would be wondering why she'd been left behind, Dave would be able to update them on the progress in the gardens...

'Oh, look!'

Toby slowed the car as the Hall came into sight.

'I know.'

He knew just how she felt on seeing that beautiful, solid, welcoming building. He knew because he felt exactly the same.

'Who's that?' she asked. 'Look, there's someone standing on the steps.'

Toby drove on, and Laurie saw that there were several people standing on the steps. Two lines of people, to be precise.

The car stopped at the foot, but Laurie couldn't move. Her eyes were rapidly filling with tears.

Sally was there to welcome them, and Dave and all his hard-working team. Terri was there, too.

'Talk about the welcoming party!'

With her vision blurred by tears, she climbed out of the car and straightened her skirt.

When she looked up, it was to see Kingsley Hall's new butler standing in front of her.

'Welcome home, Mrs Davis,' he said, bowing slightly.

'Oh!'

Too overcome to say more, she threw her arms round Dad's neck and hugged him tight.

How had he and Toby managed to keep this from her? The last she'd heard, Dad had been enjoying being back at work at the hotel!

'And you, Dad,' she said, her voice hoarse. 'Welcome home!'

'So do I still have to fire him?' Toby said, and she turned to laugh at him

'You!'

Laurie knew that Kingsley Hall would witness many more surprises in the years to come, and she could only hope they were all as wonderful as this one.

She linked arms with her father and her husband. Finally, they had come home. Home to Kingsley Hall.

This Large Print Book, for people
who cannot read normal print,
is published under the auspices of

THE ULVERSCROFT FOUNDATION